AMY KEEN

Fisher King Publishing

Phoenix

Copyright © Amy Keen 2015

ISBN 978-1-910406-08-3

Cover illustration by Chris Hyder

Fisher King Publishing Ltd
The Studio, Arthington Lane
Pool-in-Wharfedale,
LS21 1JZ
England.

Acknowledgements

Thank you to everyone who has
Read this far and continues to want
to follow Scarlett's journey.

There are no words to
express my gratitude.

For Isla

You weren't here when this story
started and now I cannot imagine
anything without you.
You are pure joy.

PREFACE

From the darkened isolation of my dream state she pleaded; always open-mouthed, silent screams, desperate attempts to communicate to me what was coming. With each vision the life force within her dimmed; the images became harder and harder to decipher and I felt an echo within me of the tug on her soul as she fought the end. Her body was weak and she was relying on her mind to complete the relay of information she had worked so selflessly to ensure I found.

In a universe where monsters existed, it seemed only reasonable to believe in the balance; that there must too be light in the world and if that was the case and fairy tales could be real, then she had to be my good witch, my fairy godmother. I reached for her within the darkness, her hand mirrored mine. At one point our outstretched fingers grazed one another with the slightest of touches causing the air to run cold as ice. It sent a blast of a chill through my entire body which woke me with a nervous start.

I felt Jake's hand press down on my shoulder. He was sleeping too and he brushed against my skin with instinctive contact before he slipped back into his own dreams. I prayed they were better, simpler than mine and that whatever it was in his head still held hope and the chance for light within our future together. I had to believe that between us there could be salvation from this nightmare as the darkness within threatened to consume me. I didn't want my soul's light to be extinguished by this witch hunt the way I knew Alice's had been. For now she remained like a fading beacon reaching out to direct me but soon, either by force or through her own will, her strength to go on would be extinguished and my guiding light would be no more.

ANOTHER CITY

The strobe effect of the street lights flashed by through the van's darkened windows and the intermittent flickering stirred me from another broken sleep. It was late and I knew we were within Amsterdam's city limits; I recognized the architecture. Endless, tall thin buildings were compressed together along the banks of canals punctuated with bridges and mechanical spider webs of bikes chained together, stretched along the sidewalk.

I propped my chin up on my hand to improve my vantage point on the street beyond. A couple, no more than a few years older than Jake and I, stumbled drunkenly along the waterside. She had fashionable, white blond hair piled high on her head and she wore denim hot pants and a vintage Rolling Stones vest cut off at the shoulders. Her slender arms were wound around the boy's waist and locked shut at the hands; she was holding on to him, claiming him and he reciprocated with a long, lingering kiss before they dissolved into hysterics at some unspoken joke to which the rest of the world were excluded. I was jealous; my insides burned with envy for them, for all their freedom to love each other without constraint or the burden of responsibility. To love with abandon, without threat - that was my dream for us.

I was jolted from my hazy reverie-cum-weird voyeuristic spying by a loud, tinny drum beat reverberating through the van's speakers and my heart leapt; I was becoming adept at jumpiness and hysteria. Jake shifted up suddenly and the sounds of mumbled voices below the din suggested Pierre and Celeste had been woken by it too. A coke can flew through the air at the side of my head and some loose strands of hair danced on the air's movement. It hit Elias square on the back of the head and he immediately turned down the volume of the stereo. "Hey, I am driving here." He glared at the four of us through the rear view mirror and I was struck by the advancement of the dark around his eyes. It was no longer the kind of strange, haunting dark that made him bizarrely transfixing. He looked, more, pained and, well, awful.

Pierre piped up behind me, "Yeah, and we were trying to rest before you turned on that abomination masquerading as music." His usually soft voice was tainted by an out of character air of grouchiness. Elias's eyes narrowed in the mirror.

"Oh really? You feeling a little sorry for yourself? Your nap didn't last long enough? Well, someone call the press… Jesus Christ. I have been sitting up here alone like a cab driver for the last three and a bit hours and I too am a little exhausted. If anyone is at all concerned." His gaze had thankfully moved back to the road but there was a collective air of shame that now hung in the back of the van. Pierre didn't speak, he shifted in his seat and dug out his phone for feigned distraction.

"Pull over." Jake had swung into authoritative mode. Elias ignored him and avoided looking back at him. "Elias. I said pull over. You're right. We need to switch it up. Even if only for the last leg. You will get us all killed if you fall asleep up there." He sat forward in his seat and I watched the shape of his back twist and expand as he stretched. Jake Meyer. Would he always hold this wholly, so all-consuming allure to me? My hands, completely independent of my brain, had already found the loops in his belt and I pulled his torso back into the seat and his face to mine. A short, knowing kiss that held so much promise and we were both alight.

"I'll pull over if you stop treating this van like a game of seven minutes in heaven." Elias said. Despite us having made it clear what was what, didn't like to be exposed to

Jake and I as a couple. He tolerated it but wouldn't suffer any more PDA than absolutely necessary. Only issue there was that with Jake, PDAs were always necessary, ergo, Elias was always pissed at me. The van came to a sudden halt at the side of the road and Elias leapt from his seat and slammed the driver's door behind him. Jake affectionately rubbed my knee as he moved toward the door which was waiting and open with a restless Elias on the other side. I saw the familiar chill between them as Jake passed and Elias couldn't help but sideswipe Jake's shoulder with his own. Thankfully, Jake recognized the need to keep focusing on the task in hand and let it go, which very evidently disappointed his opponent. Elias slumped into the seat next to me, his body turned in a way so that I was looking at his back. He closed his eyes and made a deep sigh as Jake pulled back onto the road.

Pierre and Celeste were silent behind me for the remainder of the journey and Elias feigned sleep to avoid talking to me. I occupied myself watching the blurred mirage of buildings and trees as they ran like watercolors into one another as we sped by. I vaguely remember the muted voice of the navigation system announcing our arrival and the longing hope that this was the right thing we were doing.

"Celeste. This it?" Jake's voice filled the dead air with a question that revitalized it with all the secret hopes we had that this was going to be the progress we needed so badly.

Elias lifted his head and we spun round at the same time to hungrily receive her response, our heads almost met in the middle and we both reddened; each still harboring latent anger towards one another. I wished he would just have backed off when he had the chance. His continuous mood swings were wearing and I didn't need the guilt trip on top of everything else.

Celeste strained forward to the window and cautiously looked left to right. Her blank expression was replaced with the spread of an infectious grin across her face. "Yes. That is his office over there." She pointed at a non-descript industrial looking building with large sliding wooden doors. We were on the very edge of the civilized part of town where the clusters of beautiful buildings gave way to large, imposing structures and iron cranes were mounted along the widening canals in the distance where boats floated silently, waiting in the night for their burden of freight to be loaded or unloaded. It was still dark; we had driven through the night and I didn't want to be where we were.

"Great. Well, what are we waiting for?" Jake exited the driver's door and dragged open ours which prompted a swift, silent exit from Elias. Celeste pushed by me excitedly clamoring to get out and be reunited with her brother. She seemed positively unperturbed by the circumstances of this meeting and was jigging around on concrete like an expectant puppy. Pierre and I followed and

I tried desperately to conceal the internal fight I was having with my resident ball of angst and fear.

Celeste led us to the door and proceeded to do one of the longest, most complex and intricate knocking patterns I had ever heard. The four of us stood and watched, exchanging quizzical looks. She spun round, her eyes wide with anticipation and smiled. "Sorry, it's a little odd I know. But he insists. Kind of his thing."

We waited in tense silence and it was clear Celeste was the only one mildly excited about this tentative step forward. I heard shoes tapping across the hard floor beyond and was holding my breath. Jake's hand slipped over mine and he stroked the ridges of my knuckles with his thumb; he was promising me it was going to be ok.

The sound of locks being opened spurred every muscle in my chest to tense; that sound was almost unbearable. The last time I heard that the person unlocking them wound up dead. The image of Jacques' lifeless body, bruised and bloodied in the study, filled every inch of my consciousness and I felt sick.

Behind the door was a tall, dark-haired, male version of Celeste; they could have been twins aside from his considerable height advantage. Without a glance at the company beyond, he scooped her up in his arms and her feet were off the floor as they disappeared into their embrace. Jean, or John, whichever he was going by at the time, carefully placed her down and stepped beyond the door's frame to greet us. He shook Pierre's hand first and the usually cool exterior was shattered and replaced by a fan boy moment the likes of which I have never seen. Jean was gracious and tried to ignore Pierre's fixed stare and nervous laughter. He welcomed Elias and Jake next and I felt like there was a reason I was last; singled out again, weird Scarlett. He stepped even further out to meet my gaze and the extended hand from before was withdrawn. I felt a little panicked and, without Jake's hand in mine, I was vulnerable. I couldn't read his expression and new people made me nervous these days, but within a split second I found myself entangled in his long arms; jeez, he was strong. He held me so tight and just long enough that I started to feel a little uncomfortable. My eyes darted to Jake who shrugged, his eyes betrayed him and let slip his jealousy. Celeste stepped forward to intervene but he released me before she got to us.

"Scarlett, thank you. You saved my baby sister and for that I am in your debt. I'll do whatever I can to help you. It is the very least I can do." He hadn't completely let go; his enormous hands were gripping my upper arms and I was still immobile, and feeling awkward. I managed an uncomfortable smile before Celeste playfully batted him away, setting my arms free, which were now devoid of blood.

"No, really. She saved me. I just gave her some place to run and, to be honest, I wouldn't wish this on anyone. I am..." My eyes fell to the asphalt. "I'm so sorry. To all of you." I found myself overcome with the guilt that I kept trying to pretend wasn't necessary and without a thought I was striding away as huge sobs twisted my chest. Alice was alive after God knows how long in their torturous hands; Celeste couldn't go back to Paris; Elias had sent his sister into hiding, and Jake was following me around all in the hope that there was an answer. In my moments of weakness I sometimes fought the desire to concede and say there wasn't one. I wiped the tears from my eyes as footsteps approached from behind. Jake wrapped his arms around my waist and buried his head into the nape of my neck and without a word, managed to banish the dark. We stood, silent, and stared at the industrial infrastructure beyond; both of us silently contemplating the call of the water and its promise of distance from all this. The air blew cold and he pulled me back. Celeste and the rest of the group had moved inside and the glow of warehouse lights was enticing in its contrast.

There was definitely a theme occurring with the buildings I found myself in of late; there seemed to be an abundance of structures with the odd juxtaposition of a mysterious, nondescript exterior that shrouded hyper-contemporary interiors. First there had been Elias' apartment with its futuristic locks, then the catacombs and the Venari clinical den, now this.

Essentially an industrial boathouse, the building inside

was a complex, well-appointed office set-up that looked reminiscent of some uptown, fashionable marketing agency. The air smelt of fresh coffee and new plastic. Huge silver frames containing vintage advertising prints lined the white, painted wooden walls gallery-style. The room was bright and the roof was pitched about thirty feet up where gleaming steel girders stretched from the shape of the ceiling to the horizontal bar that supported the walls. The metal was crafted presumably to a sensible, perfectly standard engineering principle, but the fact the metal spelled out a series of 'V' shapes did not go unnoticed. Their ability to infiltrate all aspects of my life was never ending. I would never be free; my heart sank even further.

From what I could tell the building went far back but a partition wall cut off the office space and the solitary door to whatever was beyond remained shut. While I was busy taking in my surroundings the rest of the gang was lounging over three sprawling red leather couches below the gallery; coffees in hand, smiles on their faces and I feigned my own, desperate to fit in for a moment. Elias was the only one who wasn't lost in the joviality of this reunion; his face remained still, his mouth a hard line.

"Ok. Sorry to break up this party..." There wasn't a hint of sincerity in Elias' voice. "But... I still think regardless of how much of a celebrity you may be..." He stared at Jean with a hint of distain and I knew he was still twisted up about leaving Paris and Ava, but he could be so cold, so rude. "We still need to get some kind of actual plan together. We have no idea if they know where we are but I don't really fancy finding out if they do." Their faces all fell and the laughter that danced between them only seconds before evaporated. Elias had that effect on people but my usual frustration toward him felt more like sadness as I watched him there in an alien room looking the darkest and loneliest I had seen him, which was saying something.

Pierre dug deep and all he could pull out was his usual 'I can't handle awkward situation' look as he grasped for his phone. Celeste watched Jean intently for a reaction while Jake pulled me into him defensively. Jean stepped up and placed a hand gently onto Elias' arm. Elias withdrew and his eyes narrowed forcing Jean to hold up his hands in surrender.

"Elias, right?" Jean sat back down as he waited for a response. "Elias, I know a little about what you guys have been through from Celeste, but I know that it is just the tip of the iceberg. I know you don't want to be here and I know..." Elias walked forward so his black boots met Jean's sneakers toe-to-toe.

"You don't know anything. Nothing about me, or her," I didn't even need to open my clenched eyelids to know his outstretched finger was pointing to me. "Or what we have been through and, yeah, I'll say what I am pretty sure they are thinking. That this little multimedia empire you think you have here isn't going to be enough. They are too many, too powerful and... forget it. You won't listen to me anyway." He stomped back to the door and slammed it behind him. Jean looked to Celeste for reassurance that it wasn't his fault and she smiled awkwardly. Jake released me and offered himself into the conversation and it felt like he was taking the lead.

"Look, Jean... I am sorry. Elias is a little volatile at times, it isn't personal. If it makes you feel any better, he hates me too." A smirk passed from Jake to Jean. "But, his attitude aside, he does have a point. We don't know what they are doing right now and we need to move forward with our side of the plan." I moved to level with Jake and thread my fingers through his hands at his side.

"That isn't strictly true." Before the words had left my mouth my lungs were constricting at their meaning. Their four faces turned to mine in unison, all of them painted with confusion.

"What do you mean, Scarlett?" Jake's voice had lost its confidence and his puzzled eyes bore into mine.

"On the way here I had a vision, no, a dream actually, but I know, I know it was real and I can't explain how, you just have to trust me." I listened to my body's declaration of weakness and sat to avoid a fall. "Alice is alive. They are using her to trace me. That is how they have known so much about me all this time; they never killed her. They kept her alive and imprisoned to get to me." Celeste and Jean looked at each other as they tried to piece it together.

Neither of them knew who Alice was but I saw the flash of recognition in Pierre's face as he slotted the puzzle into place.

"Why didn't you say something?" Jake stood between me and the rest of the group with his eyes fixed on me like it was just us there. "Scarlett? Why didn't you tell me what you saw?" He was so hurt, I could see it in his eyes. It was like blasphemy to deny him the chance to comfort and protect me; he couldn't cope with being in the dark and I knew I would feel the same. The guilt twisted in me and I stroked his blindingly beautiful face with the back of my hand.

"I was working through it for myself. I am learning how to focus, how to use all this... this stuff I have now. I think if I clear my head I can talk to her or at least hear what they want, what they plan to do next. But I need to be more cantered, relaxed. Right now I am too exhausted; I need to eat and get some sleep. And I need to see that he is ok." My eyes flashed guiltily toward the door and Jake rolled his eyes in my periphery.

"You should have told me about Alice." His voice was hushed but he was pissed.

"I'm sorry," I whispered. The others looked around uncomfortably before Celeste struck up some lame conversation about the décor as a diversion. "I didn't want everyone to be... well like this." I looked round at their consciously averted eyes. "All uncomfortable and expectant. I don't know yet what I can do with that... or any of the other stuff, not to any useful extent. That is why we are here, remember?" He nodded solemnly; his eyes were avoiding mine too. He had his arms folded defensively across his middle and I was aching to touch him and make it better. I couldn't handle any tension between us, it threw me totally off. More off if that were at all possible.

I placed my hand on his arm and tugged at his sleeve; my olive branch, I played the affection card. It worked. He didn't look at me, but he placed his hand on mine and his thumb instinctively rubbed my skin and it burned. He pulled me to him and kissed my hair as a sigh escaped his mouth. I was so tempted to fall into him and just let him hold me but I was distracted by Elias' absence. I shot Jake a look which communicated my intentions and simultaneously asked for his blessing. He released me gently from his grasp and I pretended not to see the sadness in his eyes as I turned to leave and find Elias.

The warmth of the lights inside made the sensation of rushing cold air hitting my skin even harsher; I retreated into myself, my arms hurriedly folded across my body and my neck hunched into what warmth I could find inside my collar. I saw him standing by the water's edge and I knew he knew I was there, hell, even if he hadn't heard the door he would have sensed it, I am sure. I couldn't fight the thought we were more similar than he was willing to share and I had trouble believing that listening was his only gift. There was just something about the way he sometimes looked at me as well as all the odd, inexplicable moments we seemed to share. He was so complicated, so deep and unnerving.

The watery reflection of lights danced on the canal as I approached. I watched as he moved slowly and wearily into a sitting position so his legs hung down towards the water. I sat alongside him and felt a twinge of hurt, or maybe wounded ego, as he flinched at the moment our arms grazed one another. I didn't speak. I didn't really know what to say. I was kind of angry; I had given him opportunity after opportunity to extricate himself and he stayed of his own free will, yet continued to act like such an ass. In contrast I felt pity, he was so sad and he wasn't even trying to hide it now. I wanted so badly to know what it was that weighed on him, beyond all the obvious things that were happening all around us. This was bigger than The Venari and the current situation and it had been building for a while. I tried to remember the airport stranger version of him; the one who was all loud French attitude and smiles and it was almost physically painful to try marrying that fading image with the shadow of a boy who sat beside me now.

"What are you doing out here, Scarlett? I am sure Jake would rather you were inside wrapped around him." It was going to be one of those kinds of exchanges. I sighed as I contemplated my next move. "Don't be like that, Elias. It doesn't suit you." I tried to force his gaze and his surrender but he stared off toward where the canal widened determined not to give in. "While I am getting used to your attitude dysfunction, I kind of hope it isn't here to stay." The corners of his mouth curled slightly and I knew I had taken the lead in this game, but his eyes still stayed away from mine and focused hard on a distant boat. "Please." It was a shameless plea.

"What?" There was an attitude shift, his head spun and his sudden gaze, the gaze I had been trying to provoke, took me by surprise. His face was alarmingly close and I felt like it was bordering on the uncomfortable, given past situations. I shifted slightly away and a venomous hiss escaped through his clenched teeth. I had lost again. "See, this is it, Scarlett. You want to know, you want to help but you are so god damned concerned with what he thinks that you are scared to mean it. To really know." I wasn't sure if I knew what he meant and I was ignoring it or if the confusion I felt was based on an unpleasantly intoxicating combination of realization and the sense that this conversation may head down a road I didn't want to travel. A nervous ball of energy knotted in my stomach which was already pretty crowded with all manner of fear and anxiety. I exhaled a breath I hadn't realized I was holding and absorbed some of the silence that sat like stone cold concrete between us.

"I do want to know. I want to know all sorts of things." I pulled my hair nervously into a knot to keep it from my face and held his gaze. "I want to know why you keep staying when you obviously don't want to. When you could walk away. I want to know why you get so angry and why it scares me like something bigger is happening that you aren't telling me. I want to know why you and I can't quite seem to get on... I could go on forever, Elias, really." I had found my voice and he was surprised. His intention had obviously been to warn me off and he had expected me to leave him there. Still riding high on my unexpected burst of coherent and direct speech meant I had no intention of giving him the satisfaction.

"OK. You really want to know some stuff?" He was challenging me. I straightened my back and renewed my glare in preparation while I fought desperately to stop the rising wave of stress from showing in my face. Somewhere deep inside my subconscious was screaming 'bring it on' but it trailed off into a pathetic whisper and the conviction faded with it.

"Yes, Elias. I really want to know." I raised an eyebrow with feigned confidence and his eyes narrowed.

"Ok. Yes. I could have and probably should have gone ages ago. Ava is in hiding because I stayed and all I get is the supporting role in your drama. It isn't enough and I hate it. What was next... oh, yeah. I am so angry. Well, yes, yes I am. Pretty angry."

"Elias, that isn't fair." He looked up at me through his hair. "I told you to stay. To stay with Ava." His position shifted and his defenses dropped. His body faced me openly and I avoided an obvious retreat by simply pulling my coat tighter.

"I was scared for you, Scarlett. I still am. This whole thing just keeps growing and growing and I want an end to it too. I want to be here for you but you make it so damned hard."

"I make it hard?" I was surprised to say the least by his accusation.

"Yes. Impossible in fact. I have waited my whole life to find someone I felt I could talk to about all this mad stuff. Pierre, The Collective, it helps, but it isn't enough. They don't hate it like I hate it. They don't resent it. They think all these powers are gifts. Well, I don't. I feel cursed and that fear you talk about, about the dark in me. You're right." His eyes were alight with some form of dark energy; they were luminescent orbs in his pale face. "I am dark."

I placed a hand on his arm and this time he didn't move away. He was so still but his eyes were glowing with anticipation or emotion and were hard fixed on my face. I flushed at the proximity and closeness I had naively initiated. "You aren't dark, Elias. You are a good person. It is ok to resent it, I do. I want nothing more than to be normal and hang out and simply be, without all of this. But, you know what...? We are here, this is what we have been dealt and we have a responsibility now to do something. Well, not you so much, but I do. You still have a choice." He laughed insincerely.

"Scarlett. They killed my parents. Both of them. I have my own axes to grind here. It isn't all about you." I pulled my hand back, wounded and so sad for him. I had guessed as much along the way; the way it was just him and Ava, his anger and determination to be part of this but I hadn't been sure. He knew the price of playing a part in this too well and my heart broke for him. Physical pain swelled in my chest but his attitude toward me stopped me from reaching out the way I yearned to do.

"Jesus, Elias. I know it isn't. You are such a split personality at times. One second you need me to talk to, the next you are accusing me of being too self-involved to understand you. Make up your mind. I came out here to see if I could help but you know what? Maybe you need to be alone." I started to stand but he halted my progress as he pulled me back to sit alongside him. One hand still on my sleeve he thrust the other to shield his eyes. Shield them so I wouldn't see his tears.

"I'm sorry. Scarlett, I am so sorry. I feel like I am losing it. Please don't go. Please." His words were faint, weak and filled with grief. I gave way to my instinct and pulled him into my arms in a fierce embrace, something I knew he needed. I felt the burning desire to check behind me, terrified in case Jake saw and took it the wrong way, but

Elias would flip, he was too delicate. I had to put him first at that moment.

He let go. I felt the release of muscles in his back and his shoulders as the tension unfurled at my touch. I was shocked and scared by my effect on him. I knew I was on dangerous ground. As the silent sobs rippled through our united torsos I leaned my head on to his and inhaled his scent. He was still Elias from Paris; alcohol and cigarettes were his trademark and I smiled at some of our earliest encounters. He wiped his face with the back of his sleeve and sat up. "Shit. I am so embarrassed. Please don't tell them. Him. What happened out here." I extended my pinkie finger and we dissolved into a childish giggle as he hooked his own into mine, but the underlying bitterness he inferred about Jake clung in the air – at least for me.

"Swear." The silence crept back and he was still staring at my face intently. His hand grabbed me purposefully and he wound his fingers through mine. His touch didn't burn like Jake's but I left it there, I didn't stop him. I figured this was ok and I frantically buried the heady combinations of feeling that this was stirring in me. I was so drawn to him, so protective but I didn't feel for him the way I was becoming surer he did for me. I didn't have that same attraction and intoxication I felt with Jake. For me at least, Elias and I were not beyond the slightly intense plutonic; but I wanted, maybe needed, him around. He did understand the darkness, the fight and it felt good to have

21

that balance in my life regardless of the complications it brought.

His face moved closer to mine and his breath warmed the cold skin on my face. His eyes closed as he exhaled a slow, controlled breath. I was paralyzed. His eyes stayed shut and my head began to crackle and fizz. With his head just inches from mine he was communicating with me; silently, secretly.

Scarlett. If you can hear me right now squeeze my hand. I responded. *I have to say some of this and I feel like this is the best way. Like it never happened, but at least then you know and I can let go of some of the thoughts that just keep plaguing my mind over and over.* Even his internal voices were melancholy.

Elias please, don't. I squeezed his hand again and rested my other on top.

Don't say anything else. I am sorry if this is selfish but I don't care. Please. I had conceded in my silence and he gripped me tighter. *I don't know if we can win this.* He sounded like Jacques had that night, not long before they killed him. *Maybe we won't. I don't know. But I am here, for you, and I want to try. There is something about you. I don't know what it is but I felt it from the very first time I saw you at the airport and I know you feel it too. You feel something around me, don't you?* I couldn't move and the odd feeling in my stomach spread to my chest and my cheeks. I closed my eyes to focus. *Don't you?* He pressed.

Did I? Guilt, fear, a sad longing to want to say whatever would make him feel better coursed through me. *...but it's not...*

...I know it's not the same for you. But I need to know that I am not crazy, that there is something.

Yes. There is something. For me it is just... He cut me off again. I knew he didn't want my explanation, he wouldn't like it. I was grateful for the interruption. It felt wrong to even admit in our minds that I had this weird connection with him. It was as if the admission was adultery and I felt sick with the taste of betrayal.

I know, Scarlett. He was mad. I opened my eyes briefly and took in his pain. It was etched all over his face; his dark features were screwed tight and his jaw clenched. *You love him. I get that. I am not that much of a jerk. I just needed to hear you say it. But this is hard for me. Because on my side of it all, I have to watch you play it all out with him and wish it was me.* It felt like my heart was literally falling apart. I stroked his hand with my fingers and brought them to my mouth. I placed a sad, apologetic kiss on the back of his hand and placed it back in his lap. He wouldn't release my grip and instead pushed his fingers further through mine. The space in our mind was quiet for a moment, both of us processing and dealing with our own feelings.

I am sorry, Elias. I don't know what else to say.

You don't need to say anything. It has helped just to say

it out loud, or whatever.

I wanted to move but, as if he heard the synapses in my brain click into action, he stopped me. *Wait. Can I just...? Please. I need one thing.* I held my breath. Before I could ask my question I felt his mouth on mine. It wasn't to tempt me; it was to pour out his hurt and longing. I should have moved but I didn't. I let his lips move on mine for a second, so softly and I raised my hand to his chest and pushed him lightly away. I didn't need to speak. He knew I wouldn't reciprocate but I already had untold guilt and weirdness to process. I needed to get to Jake and absolve myself of this moment. In a strange way I felt glad he had kissed me because it cleared up the niggling wonder and fear I had about how he made me feel. It proved to me that I didn't want him that way and I was glad to be free of the confusion, but it caused me to burn with a different kind of feeling; he was here and he mattered to me, in an unknown but complicated way.

Our eyes opened in perfect unison and he released my hand without prompting. I smiled at him and noticed the alarming glow and fear from his eyes had been extinguished. Whatever had just happened had helped him in some way. His index finger traced the line of his bottom lip as I stood and he recalled that moment our lips were together. We didn't say another word. I turned into the wind and allowed it to blow a little of the tension away as I headed back with eyes still blurry from being closed for so long.

The fuzziness dissipated suddenly and my heart-rate spiked at the sight of a silhouette illuminated in the doorway. I couldn't see who it was and I was filled with burning panic. My pace picked up to answer the questions my eyes were raising. Who was it? How long had they been standing there there? Then just please, God, not Jake; not like this.

REVELATIONS

The wind had picked up and was blowing my hair across my face. I swept it back, desperately willing my eyes to clear. My heart dropped to the floor and my legs threatened to follow. The silhouette was moving closer to me with long, determined strides.

"Celeste?" My eyes were glad to see her walk into view. The look on her face showed she was puzzled but not judgmental. Maybe she hadn't seen anything.

"Scarlett, we are heading off back to Jean's now. You two need to get back here so we can make a move." If she had seen anything she wasn't giving anything away.

"Celeste I…" I outstretched a hand to stop her turning from me and she stared at me with some deep, unspoken promise.

"I know. It's all good. You don't have to say anything. Let's just go shall we?" She smiled and I knew then she had seen enough but she was on my side. Elias wasn't exactly subtle in normal circumstances so she probably wasn't even shocked. I just hoped it was clear that it was him and not me, but any attempts to further qualify events would only add to my feeling and probably look of guilt. How apt my name sounded in the circumstances. Scarlett woman.

Inside, Jean was packing his laptop and some papers into a large, officious looking hold-all while Pierre and Jake were fiddling with some gadgets on one of the sprawling desks. Jake turned; his face still fraught with tension and beckoned me to him. I nestled into his arms with the hot weight of recent events pressing in my gut. I had to tell him soon; I had to before his lips touched mine again. His embrace was more forced and rigid than usual and the strange air between us was electrified with added intensity as Elias sashayed in like nothing had happened. I felt like there was a neon sign above my head announcing it all to the group and Celeste, intuitive as ever, caught my line of sight and motioned for me to take a deep breath. I followed her orders and moved my lips to Jake's ear.

"Can I talk to you? Alone." His answer was the action

as he turned toward the door and pulled me behind him, careful to go out of his way and bump Elias' shoulder. I felt his eyes watch us as we left; their hot imprint on the back of my head suggested he knew full well what I was doing and he did not approve. This had the potential to go very badly.

The cold air shocked me again as we waited for the door to fully close. His head hung low and though he still held my hand in his it was like he was miles away. I pulled his chin up with my index finger and fought the urge to kiss his slightly parted lips. The hair on the top of his head, where it was longer, blew in the wind and I wanted to run my fingers through it and tell him I loved him.

"Elias is…" He scoffed at the mention of his name.

"Of course it is about him. It is always about him…." The air was green with his potent jealousy and the threat of what I had to tell him was lodged in my throat like a dagger. One headed for his weakness; the part that loved me.

"Please, Jake. Listen. He is really struggling. We need to give him time and just be there for him. You included." His face was up but his eyes looked anywhere but at me. "The Venari killed his parents. He is lonely and scared."

"Are you that naïve, Scarlett? He is feeding you all of this to get you to feel sorry for him. Like we don't all have our own sob stories? My dad is dead. I killed him. He was a monster who tried to kill you. You have had to escape.

Twice. His is hardly the only sadness in our little group of misfits."

He was right. We all had our problems but Elias wasn't coping with his and my protectiveness over him was going to continue to raise its head time and again.

"Please, Jake. Please go easy on him, for me." Finally his eyes met mine and he stared directly into me. He nodded reluctantly, defeated. Our heads instinctively gravitated towards each other; our open mouths answering some silent siren call, but I stopped as I felt a sudden rush of emotion. My eyes glazed over and my lower lip quivered with my forthcoming confession. "There is something else…" It was my turn to look down. I drew in a deep, almost painful breath knowing that when I released the words I wouldn't be able to take them back. On bringing them back up his own eyes looked overcome with fear like he knew and was already broken.

"He kissed you, didn't he?" His words were a blade into my soul. His pain echoed through the air and through his touch into my own hand. The worst was the lack of anger or surprise in his voice. I nodded solemnly.

"Jake. I didn't kiss him back. He is messed up. He needed to get a lot out of his system and it… I don't know. But it was a second and I am only telling you because I don't want there to be secrets. I want you to trust me. To know you can trust me. Totally. Always." I was unable to stop the torrent of apologetic, pleading words from escaping.

"Say something. Please." The silence twisted the knife of guilt further. I grabbed his other hand and pulled him toward me.

"I trust you." He whispered the words and a tidal wave of relief washed over me. "But I don't forgive him. Twice he has overstepped the line and I won't be made a fool of, Scarlett." Wounded pride; the real and lasting issue here. "I swear to God, I will not let this go again and you'll forgive me if I don't let you run after him next time he has a toddler tantrum."

I wouldn't succumb to being minded the entire time but for now conceding was better than fighting. He loved me still. He trusted me. I had done the right thing.

"I understand. I will make sure he stays in line. Jake, I am so, so, sorry." The tears streamed down my face and the test of his forgiveness came as he leaned into me and kissed them from my cheeks. His hands were either side of my face and he moved his lips to my mouth where I was breathless in anticipation of a kiss. A passionate, longed-for kiss that spelled out in a second everything that made him right for me. I burned with desire and a deep-rooted love that I could barely articulate. He brought every element of me alive.

Our foreheads came together and we shared the same breath as he looked at me and kissed each cheek once more. "No more tears. This wasn't your fault and I know you were worried to say it. Please don't be scared to talk to me. The idea of you fearing anything about me is terrible."

"I'm not scared of talking to you. I am scared of losing you. I've told you before. Not many people would put up with this kind of crap as it is. I just needed you to be sure of how I feel about you. No-one can change that. Ever." His lips smiled as they pressed against mine.

Pierre cleared his throat alongside me and we moved apart, both slightly flushed at being busted, but our hands remained entwined. He was flanked by a very dark looking Elias and I witnessed a certain look between he and Jake and exhaled with relief at its brevity. If that was the only fallout from what happened I had done really well with the damage limitation.

Elias turned and threw some stuff back into the van, where Celeste was already waiting. I climbed in behind Jake and Pierre followed, choosing to sit up front with Elias. Jean disappeared out of my line of sight and his return was heralded by a deep, rumbling motorcycle engine. Of course the new media celebrity had a motorcycle. What else? Elias spun us round and we followed the red glow of his tail light back into civilization.

Amsterdam was alive, and beautiful. It was always a place on my list; naturally, I hadn't imagined the kind of circumstances that would bring me here. I was thinking more city break, cultural getaway than hiding out with some guerrilla media hotshot, but in the fleeting moments I caught sight of the architecture or one of the canals through the van window I allowed myself to pretend I was on vacation instead.

After a half hour winding through the streets we entered a network of narrow, claustrophobic back roads that put Elias on edge. He kept cursing about his mirrors and their proximity to the walls while Jean nipped nimbly left and right leaving us to chase his afterglow. It looked decidedly less appealing than the waterside properties we had passed. Huge commercial waste containers and garbage sacks were piled against grubby painted walls, while dim lights flickered ominously over shattered tarmac. We wound round such tight corners left and right that I started to feel dizzy; so it was a relief when we stopped. I had closed my eyes for the last ten minutes to abate the dizziness and apparently missed the transition from urban wasteland to city hideaway.

We pulled up in a courtyard at the bottom of a typically tall, thin building bursting with, seemingly, endless levels and lines of wooden framed windows. We had been enveloped within its confines by a wall, probably six feet tall, and large wooden gates which were still moving electronically to a close when I looked up. The contrast was startling.

The van door slid open and Jean looked in, helmet under his arm and smiled. "Home. Sweet. Home. Let's go." We piled out like eager children and filed in behind him as he unlocked the door. The hallway stretched in each direction; the contemporary solid wood floor softly reflected the light of a low hung and expensive chandelier. It was ultra- modern, shards of shaped glass like icicles in a whirlpool formation. It was stunningly beautiful but looked alarmingly dangerous, especially to Jake and Jean, whose heads barely cleared its drop.

"Welcome. Enjoy. The guest bedrooms are on the second floor. They are all made up and you each have your own bathroom where you'll find towels, robes and all that stuff." Celeste was smiling broadly at the open-mouthed awe etched across all of our faces. "Go, make yourselves at home and I will get some food started. Explore, shower. Mi casa es su casa." With that Jean headed down the hall toward the back of the house where the start of an epic, most-likely catering size, kitchen was just visible. This house was incredible.

The stairs were dressed in a coarse, patterned carpet that was charcoal grey and accented with a gallery of frames that lined the walls. Pictures of Amsterdam, of Jean and Celeste, people I presumed were their parents and some news clippings about Jean's viral video. This place just went on and on. The first floor hinted at even more super-slick décor but with doors ajar I couldn't see all the way into the rooms. Jake and I led the ascent to the guest floor and assessed the bedrooms one by one. We got first pick again, which worked out well as we clinched the suite at the front of the house which was all pale, dove grey this time. The carpet was inches thick and felt like clouds, a huge bed was framed by vintage-looking, extending wall lights and two matching acrylic side tables that almost disappeared into the white walls behind the bed-head. It didn't have that Slightly Less Important Room So Less Impressive feel, this was a room that had benefitted from all the design TLC you would expect to pay five hundred dollars a night for. Jean was a media magnate with taste.

Jake and I shared a smug smile; this was almost perfect. If we could just find a way to free the entire Collective from the grasp of The Venari then we would be all set. Yeah, simple as.

The duvet enveloped me as I fell onto the bed and Jake collapsed beside me. My eyes closed; I absorbed the sounds that emanated from downstairs. Jean was clattering around in the kitchen while Celeste was singing to herself on the floor below. Pierre and Elias were silent, no doubt catching up on some sleep, or in Elias' case, brooding and listening. He hadn't spoken to me on the journey over, or even when our arms brushed in the hall as we arrived. His bedroom choice had been a floor below us and the other end of the house – maximum distance meant minimum chance of butting heads with Jake, who had made it perfectly clear there would be no more free passes for Elias' crappy behavior. I still couldn't bring myself to feel angry at him; the kiss, the weird conversation, it had only served to enlighten me on how lonely and sad he was. I kept my thoughts to myself; that conversation only ever went one way. Instead, I freshened up, took Jake's hand and led him down to the source of the noise.

In the kitchen, which was even bigger than I had anticipated, Jean was fiddling with a complex looking oven while Celeste sat on a stainless steel counter that was as wide as it was long, her legs were swinging happily. What was it with guys living alone and this obsession with steel? I could see she had already lost herself in this presence, this little idyll we were trying to create – just friends casually gathering for a meal in this absurdly palatial townhouse while they were plotting and doing god knows what to poor Alice in order to get to me. Totally normal to be in this much denial.

"Smells so good," I purred the words, I was suddenly starving. "What are we having?" I looked to Jean who was now stirring a monster pot of something and humming to himself. He padded toward me, a wooden spoon in his hand which he thrust unceremoniously into my mouth. My god, it was the best chili I had ever tasted in my life. "Wow." He smiled and returned to the stove. Impressive, a great cook, a huge house and a media genius. It was as if my thoughts were aloud as Elias and Jake rolled their eyes almost in unison, feeling defeated by Jean's accomplishments. I smirked at their immaturity; guys were jerks.

Celeste hopped down excitedly, "Scarlett, come with

me. I need to show you the rest of the house." There was more? She grabbed my hand and led me to the back of the kitchen where the room opened further into an amazing dining space which was dominated by an enormous wooden table with two fashionable benches that ran the length of it. The center of the table was marked with a glass bowl maybe two feet in diameter; the kind of thing that probably cost more than everything I owned but was completely wasted on me. My family weren't the interiors types; we had nice things and our house in Washington had always looked normal. Pleasant, but never stylish or fashionable. Mom's nature led her to choose battered, well-worn antiques over the kind of furniture that graced Home and Living magazine, and even then, not the kind of antiques that would ever bear the 'eco-cycling' or vintage crazes.

I hadn't even realized I had stopped until Celeste tugged on my hand and pulled me through a gap she was holding with her foot in a pair of waxed wooden doors. "Come see this." She yanked my body into the space she had occupied moments before and we found ourselves in what could only be described as a gadget-freak's wet dream. The room in front of me would probably have loosely slotted into the outer-limits of the description of an office, though I had never seen one outside of fancy corporations on the TV be so well-equipped. Jean certainly had a thing for the slightly grandiose. Celeste hadn't spoken yet; she was reclining in a high-backed white leather chair that rotated loosely on a silver pedestal, her face alight with sibling pride. Her chair was situated behind a black high-gloss desk that ran for more than five feet along the left hand side of the room. There was a wall of TV screens to the right and I felt a cold shudder run though me, as the memory of Paris flooded my senses. Sutcliffe leaning over me with that sickly sweet grin on his face when the extent of my powers began to manifest itself before his eyes like he had always planned. Sick freak. A renewed desire to beat them rose up in my throat, but I pushed it down, ready to focus on the now for just a little longer.

"This is pretty impressive," I scoffed. I didn't really know what else to say. Wait. This was better than just technology. Yes, there were maybe ten generations of Apple products on the desk and the screens suggested serious co-ordination of important media activity, but, the back wall. How had I not noticed it before? Books. Row upon row of beautiful books encased in a floor to ceiling case; perfectly lit and calling to me. My face lit up; that scent of paper. Now I had seen them I became acutely aware of my desire to stand there in front of them, touch them, read them – all if I had the opportunity. I flashed Celeste a look and she gestured for me to explore; she was now illuminated by the glow of an unsurprisingly ostentatious widescreen monitor as her fingers tapped furiously on the ultra-slim keyboard, naturally.

I advanced until I was close enough that I had to crane my neck to look up to the top rows. I needed a library like this. Even more pleasing than the overall sight of them was the content. Jean had every great work of literary fiction I could think of and then some. The old and the new seamlessly coordinated in one perfect space. Of course, there were some books of no interest to me whatsoever; I mean the books on computing and self-help weren't my thing. I wanted escapism, not instructions. Maybe it was a weird sign that all these people I kept being led to - Jacques, Jean - they all had libraries and seemed like they held the key to the whole damn mess. They suggested that knowledge really might be power.

"Is Jean, you know… like, totally self-made? Did he really teach himself all this stuff?" I could hear Celeste's fingernails still tapping on the keys.

"Yes. He struggled being social when he was younger. Ironic, no? A few years locked away teaching himself how to master the art of the internet and some sociology and look at him now. Isn't this house the most amazing place you've ever seen?" Still lost in my tome nirvana, I nodded, without giving any thought at that time to whether or not she would have been able to see my response.

"Yeah. Amazing." I answered the call of a particularly beautiful poetry collection and brought it to my nose. That paper smell, there was really nothing like it. "Celeste?" My voice was heavier now with the weight of the impending question. "Do you really think all this, everything he knows, Jean, will be enough to help me?" I sensed a slight dimming in the light behind me as the monitor shutdown and Celeste appeared beside me.

"I do. I really do. And I am not just saying that. He is good at what he does and somehow we will figure out a way to make that work for you. But, Scarlett, seriously, the real reason I feel confident is you." She linked her arm through mine and gave my wrist a tentative squeeze. "You can do this. Look how far you have come. I barely know you, but I know I trust you and I know you are more powerful than you give yourself credit for. So even if you are terrified, or don't believe it yourself... know that we do. We can just see it. There is something inside you, Scarlett." Inside me? There was a little too much going on for my liking. She sensed the contraction of my muscles. "I don't mean anything bad." Had she read my mind? "What they are showing, by going to all these lengths to get to you is that you are better and bigger than they are. They know it and we will exploit every weakness they have. Together." She squeezed my wrist again and exhaled a slow, contemplative breath.

"Why would you even do this for me? Honestly. I mean I bring this horrendous, irreversible chaos into your life, and now your brother? Why?" I almost felt the dejection in the air. She had hoped her rousing speech would send me into a motivational tail spin and I would have to be brought down from my high about my readiness to get up and fight.

"Because I have spent my life being weak, Scarlett. I took their money when I knew something bad was happening. This is my way of putting it right, of doing something useful. Jean too. He wants to help; this isn't some misplaced obligation or favor to me. His passion is using information that people deserve to know to bring down the bad guys. Sometimes that's politicians, sometimes its CEOs of huge, blood-sucking corporations and, ok, this is a little different but this time it is bringing an end to the tyranny of some sicko society." Her mouth spread into a wide smile and she wiped a tear from my cheek that I hadn't even realized I had shed. The lump in my throat was so tight I couldn't speak so I mouthed a thank you at her and turned to leave.

The doors back to the kitchen swung open and a waft of glorious-smelling air forced the scent of books and the thoughts of them away. Jake stood there, his hair backlit and the curve of his arms distracting as he held the door. Celeste crept awkwardly beneath his arm revealing perhaps a little more than she would have hoped that his presence made her, like many other girls, a little nervous. I stopped at his frame, my chest against his and pressed a soft, slight kiss onto his lips. Beyond him the table was busy with plates and clanging cutlery. I was faintly aware of Elias' discomfort at our affection and I knew there was a chance he was communicating it freely but I wasn't having any of the usual interference so it may have just been the sight of his hunched, unanimated frame in my periphery. Jake smiled beneath and ushered me through. "Come on. You need to eat."

THE MESSAGE

In the morning, we congregated in the office-cum-Library of Dreams like we were reporting for duty. Jean stood officiously behind his desk and we sat awkwardly on random chairs, all bar Elias, who had taken it upon himself to lean nonchalantly against the wall of screens. That was, until Jean shot him a look and a mildly aggressive clearing of the throat sound, which made him sheepishly retreat to sit crossed legged on the floor like a kindergartener. It didn't go down well.

Anyone walking into such a room of misfits would not have believed this was The Room; the one in which we would formulate The Plan. It seemed like if that were really going to happen there should be some kind of difference, it should feel more triumphant, epic. But apart from the glorious view of the books at the end of the room and the warmth of newly drunk coffee, it was like any other room on any other day.

Jean spun in his chair like a movie villain, his fingertips touching in an arch. Elias scoffed and Celeste shot him a 'Give it Up or Die' look which he surely must have been used to by now. Coming from her it seemed to have more of an impact; mild mannered and delightful Celeste turning hard ass sent his eyes to the floor where his feet shuffled awkwardly. Pierre was quiet. He had retreated into himself a bit here; maybe he was happy not to have to lead, to keep Elias under control, now there were so many others to help with that.

"I don't know how long we have or what you know, so I guess this morning is really about making sure we all understand the situation and what can be done." Jean flashed me a concerned look and I felt his anxiety for the first time. It stirred my own. "Scarlett, Celeste has already explained to me what you can... do and obviously, from my perspective, we need to harness the whole projection thing. I need to get to grips with the scope of that so I can use it."

Elias rose to his feet, my stomach dropped. "Look, I know we talked about this in Paris and I went along with the notion but seriously? I thought we were coming here for space, to think of a real plan," Pierre motioned for Elias to sit down, his mortification at his friend's continually childish behavior was wearing thin and even his nature was being challenged. I hadn't notice Jake rise to stand behind me.

"Oh, you went along with it? As I recall you acted like a jerk and pouted the whole way here." Jake folded his arms, his eyes fast on Elias. He was seeking revenge through public humiliation.

"Scarlett, can't you keep your guard dog in line? He is pissing me off." Elias said.

Jake fuelled the fire with a sarcastic laugh which resulted in Elias' face contorting into a tense frown. I wanted to speak, to intervene, but I was tired of this, of them and their fighting. I looked round hoping someone else would step in but it seemed from the barely guarded smirks that everyone else was enjoying the show.

"Oh, you would like that wouldn't you? Me getting all up in your face so you can run to her and plead innocence? Maybe you're thinking you'll get another chance to be alone. Perhaps you think… oh, I don't know; that you can try for another pathetic, unrequited kiss?" There was a gasp, I couldn't be sure who from as I was too busy picking up my own jaw from the floor. He wasn't supposed to say anything. Elias looked at me with a look that I couldn't quite place but I was willing to hazard a guess it was betrayal, or worse, disappointment. He rose from his sitting position and I thought he might actually make the right choice and just walk away. He cleared the length of Jean's desk and almost reached the door through to the kitchen when he stopped, his back to the rest of us and dipped his head. The room was silent and felt darker somehow. I could hear the buzz of his thoughts in my head but no discernible message. It was just pure rage.

The pause seemed so long that I was certain someone had stopped time. He turned, his faced etched with a satisfied smirk that reeked of the chaos to come. Apparently I wasn't the only one feeling it. Jake moved beyond me and jerked his arm free from my attempt to hold him back. Elias let out a smug cackle before thrusting his clenched fist into the door; the resulting crack was evidenced permanently with the twisted, splintered wood angrily protruding through the paint. All eyes but mine and Jake's were on the floor, the walls, anywhere but addressing the vast ocean of tension that now existed in the room between us. Elias, still motionless bar the subtle and covert rubbing of his knuckles, proceeded to actually leave at that point. Jake stepped forward after him and I fought the urge to restrain him. I had reached a point where I couldn't be sure I didn't want to see them sort it out and if that meant some Neanderthal pissing contest, then perhaps it just needed to happen. Quite frankly, pandering to their egos was the bottom of the priority pile.

The door swung to a close behind Jake and the atmosphere instantly lifted but they could barely sit up straight for straining to listen to the hushed, hissed rumble of voices coming from the kitchen. I couldn't hear actual blood being spilled, so it had to be ok.

"Right, let's make some progress." Jean rose from the chair authoritatively and I barely caught my breath for the next three hours. He worked me like a dog or perhaps a more appropriate animal would be a rat, a giant lab rat. We sat for what felt like weeks in front of the wall of screens; trying the equivalent of first grade, rookie 'power' practice. We were so engrossed with it, me and my pitiful projections and minor-league object shifting that we failed to notice the light had ebbed away and the fashionable light fittings were now creating trippy star-like patterns on white ceiling. Jake. Where the hell was he? It had gone so quiet after he and Elias stormed out it seemed worryingly possible that one or both of them could have ended up unconscious, or dead. Jean had already stretched out and left in search of caffeine or some other kind of energy hit. I pulled myself up but a flash of unease signaled the weakness in my legs, which promptly buckled below as my vision narrowed into pinholes of hazy light. The crash of my body to the floor was accompanied by the soundtrack of Celeste screaming for Jake.

My hand stretched out to the door handle with trepidation; the simplest of things had become laced with fear for never knowing what lay in wait on the other side. I was aware of the fact that the very notion of being fearful, when what I was seeing was in the future, was ridiculous, but I felt it regardless both in the vision and in the me that existed now in a heap on the library floor. I paused at the sight of movement in my periphery; there was a small video screen on the wall to my right, an image busied in monochrome. I took a step closer to examine who or what was creating the furor of action: people, lots of people. I exhaled with relief as I realized they were in fact not at the door but at the gates, some fifty or sixty feet away. My hand turned the deadlock and I punched in the code I couldn't remember being told before the door sprang open from its electronic lock and the warm outside air rushed through my hair, which was down and falling almost to my elbows now and fanned it out around me. The waiting crowds were eerily silent and at the sight of me they fell to their knees in stunning unison behind the gates. There must have been twenty of them; all ages and nationalities, bowing, to me. More confused than usual, I urged the vision to play out further but the sense that I was losing focus crept in and the colors started to fade, my sight pixelated and the view shrunk to a pin hole of light before my eyes flickered open to the now.

As ever, I came round to find that Jake was cradling my head; his hands were stroking my hair from my face. It could only have been seconds that I was gone this time as Celeste had not yet managed to erase the look of mild hysteria from her ashen face.

"I'm fine, guys." I pulled myself up. "Ouch." The egg-sized lump on my forehead suggested a less than graceful plummet into my mind's eye on this occasion. Their expectant eyes were right on me and Celeste's screams had drawn the attention of Pierre and Elias who appeared at the same time in the doorway and fought their way in to be first to the scene.

"What did you see?" Elias showed no sympathy as ever and I watched as Jake tensed at his terse tone. "Well?"

"Back off, douche. She is still coming back from it." At this point, Jake's arms were forming a protective ring that encircled me as I sat with my knees bunched to my chest. I steadied myself by leaning on the base of the desk and he moved closer protectively. I shot him a look which no-one else may have been able to read in that space of time, but he got it and reluctantly unclenched his fist which I had clocked tightening in the corner of my eye.

I was just asking a question. I would say it was pretty relevant right now what she was seeing, wouldn't you? Elias' internal voice was not so diplomatic and I wasn't sure if it was a hangover from the vision, like some kind of power surge but his thoughts were the clearest they had ever been. The stream of expletive consciousness came to an abrupt halt, so he had obviously recognized me stowing away in his thoughts, but he didn't acknowledge it in the real world.

I fidgeted into a more comfortable sitting position and

relaxed into Jake's frame before composing my thoughts. "There are people coming." All eyes in the room focused on me intently, carrying a mix of fear and confusion.

"Wait... you need to be more specific. Who? Them?" Jake had created some slight distance between us so he could read the expressions on my face and see if he needed to be worried or not.

"Woah... woah... woah. NO!" A collective sigh filled the air, apart from Elias, who as usual was trying to look as disinterested as possible. "Not those people. People I don't know, but I didn't get a bad feeling, more confusing."

"You are not the only one who is confused Pierre. Are we expecting guests?" Celeste looked to her brother who was back in his evil mastermind chair. Jean shook his head. She bit her lip pensively and looked back to me for answers.

"I didn't get much from them but there was something really weird about it. In the vision, I opened the door and they were just there behind the gates and when they saw me they... well, they all bowed."

"Bowed?" Celeste grinned, finding it unfathomable that people could have reacted to me that way and far from being offensive, her reaction was very similar to my own.

"Yes. There were maybe twenty to thirty of them and as soon as they saw me, they just dropped to their knees. Then I was back here." Elias stood bolt upright and paced a few steps forward and back, rocking on the soles of his boots.

"This makes perfect sense. Don't you see? The Collective, I am sure it is them."

"Well I hope there are more people like us in the world than that or we really are freaks." I was on thin ice making flippant remarks to him like that; it took so little to make him turn, but then again, of all people in that room, I knew I could handle him better than anyone and so did he.

"Very funny, wise ass. I meant I bet that is why you were feeling all revered and popular. If they were people sent to help us with this master plan then you are basically their Queen, deity, God, you choose." There was a faint and almost hidden thought, something about how he would bow to me but he was trying so hard to cover it up my head ached from searching for it within his. His cheeks flushed and his eyes couldn't have sought further reaches of the room, so I think I heard right.

"Oh. Ok. Well... I think they are coming soon. I can feel all this activity in my head. It is getting busier." With that the doorbell rang and cut through the momentary silence and our eyes all met with each other. The rest of them hung back while my feet slowly carried me forward, it was instinctive; this was for me, whatever their message was, it was mine to hear. Even Jake, who normally I could rely on being entwined around me protectively, gestured for me to go alone but his body-language conveyed how tightly he was wound.

I padded through the kitchen and into the hall and felt

the strange unification of my vision world and real life as the images I was seeing perfectly matched up to the sense of deja-vu in my head. It was like slipping on glasses to help you see; all at once the things I could see made much more sense.

The monitor to the side of the door was busy in exactly the way it had been, a haze of faces just waiting expectantly. I wasn't sure if it was more or less intimidating now I knew they were here for me. My outstretched hand was trembling under the intensity of the anticipation. I unlatched the series of locks, each sound cut through silence with such force I jumped each time, even knowing it was coming. I sensed the gathering behind me; their eyes poised on me, as they hovered in the hall for a glimpse of what was coming.

When the door opened the wind carried their gasps directly to me, along with their unnervingly persistent stares. A woman at the front nearest the gates fell to her knees like this was some sort of spiritual pilgrimage and I was their God. The sense of pressure and responsibility I carried suddenly seemed more real than ever before. They wanted me to be the answer; to them, I was the answer. I finally extended my arm and pushed the door open as far as it would go. They were mumbling, hurried words passed between them from mouth, direct to ear but the hum of so many words buzzed and then faded on the breeze. I stepped out onto the house's front yard where swirling, intricate stones were laid for the drive; I hadn't even notice them as we arrived, my near constant state of distraction had seriously impacted my ability to take on board the 'normal'. If it didn't focus on a risk or pose a threat to my life then it didn't even register these days.

I moved toward the gate and silently reminded myself to breathe. My heart threatened to leap from my chest if I didn't refocus a little and my legs were already threatening to give it all up. They still weren't speaking, at least not directly to me and their looks of shock had transformed to child-like excitement. This was ridiculous and totally freaking me out.

THE ONE

It felt to me like a thousand paces to get to the gates. Weighed with anxiety my legs just dragged below me, though the entire time I found myself locking eyes with each of them in turn, still with this weird, expectant silence hanging between us. I had always hated attention, good or bad, and this fit neither of those definitions. They weren't thrilled to see me or disappointed that I was a mere mortal, more in awe of me, which somehow felt worse.

By the time I was a meter away, the tension-cum-excitement on their part was palpable. I couldn't really think of how to break the silence, other than to go with my gut which would have had me scream 'I don't know how the hell to help you' at the top of my lungs or perhaps 'you know we are probably all going to die horribly, right?'. Hardly a speech befitting of a leader of the people; though I was neither a leader nor sure who, exactly, my people were. Put simply, I was clearly not suited to public speaking, world saving or any other kind of mass assistance mission.

I was still lost in my internal monologue when I felt a hand on my shoulder. My first thought was Jake had come to stand alongside me like always, but within a split second I sense the difference in the way the hand sat, the pressure it put on me: Elias.

To my surprise and complete and utter relief, he stepped beyond me toward the waiting crowd and broke the nothing between us.

"You guys are The Collective, right?" Direct as ever. He wasn't exactly welcoming but all I could think about was how damned pleased I was that I hadn't had to speak first.

A tall, middle aged guy with salt and pepper stubble moved forward from two or three people back and took some kind of command at the head of the crowd.

"Yes. We were told she was here. This is her. This is The One, yes?" Another mysterious accent, another person likely to have been running and moving for some time, waiting for me to turn up and fix everything. Elias stiffened alongside me; knowing him the way I did, I knew he would not like me being referred to as 'her'. For all his ass-like qualities, he was sometime an old fashioned gentleman. I smiled as the memory of our first airport encounter sprang to the fore of my mind.

"She has a name, but, if you mean The One we've been waiting for then yes," he put a protective arm around me as a huge rush of enthusiasm washed among the waiting horde. "She is the one, but we are nowhere near ready yet. She doesn't have it in here to take them on." I felt suddenly deflated and a little betrayed, like he had ratted me out. Their chatter ceased and they looked between each other confused. I could see their point; you grow up a freak, berated, belittled and hunted only to be told there is hope for it all to end and for you to live peacefully, but for that to happen you need to wait for the arrival of another freak. All the above finally happens and they get me and a blank face on a doorstep in Amsterdam. This lacked a certain fairytale quality, for sure.

Something in the air changed and it felt odd, almost eerie. The spokesman motioned for them all to move back and give him space. He cracked his knuckles and closed his eyes. His hands, which I couldn't believe I hadn't noticed before as they were huge, gently moved the air around in front of the gates, a weird kind of fog followed his movements and within a matter of seconds, before anyone could react, he had pushed the ball of what I could only assume was energy forward and the huge wrought iron gates simply parted without regard for the lock that held them. Elias moved me back as the crowd surged forward and my heart started to race again. Jake appeared to my other side and I was once again flanked by my own personal bodyguards.

The man signaled for the advancing group to stop. "We are here to help. We mean no harm or threat. We can assist." Elias looked at me and I felt the cerebral click as his mind opened and he spoke freely, silently. *We can trust them.* I nodded. I guessed by now it was my time to offer something to this weird outdoor theatre show we seemed to have created.

"He's right; I'm not ready, but I will be. I promise." I have to be. The leader stood forward and shook my hand as the rest of his disciples fell to their knees in impressive unison. I quickly motioned for them to take to their feet. This was too uncomfortable and the less they behaved like I was some kind of savior, the easier it was to pretend for a moment that it wasn't all on me. By that point Pierre and Celeste had joined us on the drive and we all stood there; misfits with different problems, united by one hope for a solution. Me.

The house, just hours before had been full of latent fear and pressure for everyone, with all the extra bodies those feelings seemed consigned to just me. They were all so excited; for them gathering in that house was a huge step forward. I felt more like I was on a giant treadmill; tired, out of breath and not covering any new ground.

We found use for the huge dining table and perched like animals round a watering hole. Celeste busied herself ferrying tea and coffee and little pastries round the group while we worked through a series of normal, and then slightly less normal, introductions. First was the basic, who you were and where you were from, closely followed, of course, by what you could do. The latter was decidedly more interesting.

He, the man who opened the gates, was called Xander, which felt like it belonged to someone younger. Fifty one years old and never married, he had committed his life to harnessing his powers, learning and, as he put it, 'waiting for this moment'. It dawned on me how many lives were being lost, not in death but to the endless quest to bring some kind of peace to this forever war with The Venari. So many people who were technically off radar, free to live their lives, were throwing themselves in harm's way for a chance at justice or perhaps retribution. Not that it wasn't worthy of a fight, but, shamefully, I couldn't help but think if I had the chance to escape, I would probably take it, even now. He had been travelling around Europe for the best part of twenty years like some circus freak-cum-nomad, collecting other people who were lost and seeking a cause and, apparently, I was it.

Xander cleared his throat gruffly and stood with a brief tug on each sleeve so his plaid shirt rested just below his elbows. The people that came with him bore the same small, knowing smirk; they knew what he could do and they were excited for us to see it.

Jake pulled my hand onto his lap with a hint of anticipation for what was coming and I instinctively squeezed it back. I felt uneasy, weak compared to people who could, even without evidence, be so clearly confident in their gifts. Elias was slumped in his seat, acting disinterested but struggling not to look. Xander turned steadily, kind of eerily to face Elias, possibly down to his seeming indifference and nodded like a sensei before closing his eyes. Elias started to shift uncomfortably before a silence deeper than I had ever known engulfed the room and his posture went from apathetic to army style upright in a second. Jake looked at me and I shrugged. Elias had his eyes open but it was like he was somewhere else. I scanned the group and our other guests were most amused but Xander was perfectly still with eyes closed, motionless.

It felt like forever waiting for whatever we were watching to progress in some way. Stunned silence hung between our little group and the unease started to breed in our lack of words. I was about to ask Xander what exactly he was doing when he slowly moved his arms outwards as if he were flying. We waited and a split second behind him Elias followed suit. Xander folded his arms, Elias did too. Xander balled his hands into tight fists and sparred with the air in front of him as stubborn, moody Elias copied his repetitions exactly, without question.

My mouth gaped open as the realization dawned; Xander could control people's minds. This was insane and by far the scariest talent I had heard of yet, luckily he seemed to be a reasonable guy, but it was unnerving and made me feel vulnerable. No one had said anything in about five minutes; we were processing what this meant and all working on shutting down our minds. Elias was impenetrable for normal conversation, let alone mind control. If he could get into his head without a fight then the rest of us didn't stand a chance.

Xander lowered his arms and brushed the air in front of him away like he was swatting a fly. Elias slumped again before shaking his head and looking up, confused. His eyes found mine first which Jake noticed I am sure. He looked scared, violated.

"Wh... what the hell was that?" He moved his look, now much more a glare to Xander. He pushed himself up from the table and marched around. His hands found Xander's collar and he thrust him, back down on to the table. Xander didn't stop him or resist. "Seriously, what did you do to me?" He was shaking and angrier than I had seen him, which was saying something

Xander calmly removed Elias's hands from his collar and silently asked for permission to stand again. Elias took a reluctant step back. The knowing smiles on Xander's friends faces had waned, they were shocked by the outburst and had moved closer to one another.

"I am sorry... I meant no harm, my friend. People do not often allow me to demonstrate if they know what I can do. It is done. Please, forgive my intrusion." Xander stretched out his hand to a seething Elias. His response was to slap the hand away and two of the men from the group rose to their feet in defense. Jake put a defensive hand across my waist, knowing I was likely to spring up at any moment.

"Stay out of my head. Of all of our heads, do you hear me?" Elias looked at me, only briefly, but it was a warning. I felt the rush of activity in my head. He wasn't happy and his little thoughts about The Collective swooping in to assist had been more than shattered by this unusual episode. Xander looked mortified and for a grown man, completely stripped down. He looked to me, I shifted ahead of what I knew would only be an uncomfortable exchange.

"I feel we may have made a mistake in coming. You clearly are lucky, you have many allies here. I meant no offence." I stood out from under Jake's shield and walked round to him. I placed a hand on his. I didn't have to look to know Elias and Jake were both intently fixated on what I was doing.

"Stay. Please. I appreciate you were..." the words stopped and hung in mid-air. The strangest sensation flooded my senses from the point my hand touched Xander's there was something physical passing between us, literally flowing through my veins. I looked at him and he could feel it too, it was clear, but he didn't look weirded out, actually quite the opposite. I went to pull away as the sensation morphed into a searing burn, I winced and shifted but Xander pulled my hand back.

"Wait. Please." His eyes burned into mine and I wasn't sure whether to hold his gaze and try work out what it meant, or run. My default position these days felt like run and I was urging myself to be stronger. The feeling faded. The burn eased and his hand released mine. No one had spoken again in the longest time.

Jake rose to his feet. His chest was puffed out and I could sense without properly looking he was into protective mode. "Ok. That is enough. You turn up here, you control my friend..." Elias and I both stiffened at the use of the word friend, and while I embraced the seeming small victory, Elias offered only another eye roll as thanks. "Now you are getting all weird with Scarlett. You need to just back off a little. Tone it down. I thought you guys were supposed to help or something, not just turn up and creep everyone out."

Xander was clearly at a loss for words. He took a step back and slumped into the waiting chair. Instead of addressing Jake he stared right back at me.

"You felt it, yes?" I knew what he meant but in recent experiences the outcome was never good. I nodded. "Well, then try it."

"Try what? I don't understand?" He shook his head in

exasperation and I felt my cheeks flush. I may be some kind of savior to them but I am pretty sure another ten minutes and I would have been able to convince them otherwise. My 'none of this is going to work out' act was working and I think the newcomers all thought I was stupid or just a general lost cause, either way, their confidence was waning rapidly.

"See if it is true." Again, my mind was a blank. He read the nothing on my face and pulled up a young girl from The Collective to stand in front of me. "Try with her what I did with your friend."

"Wait… what's true? Do what? My head is freaking killing me. Pretend, if you will, that I am not some superhero sent to save you and in fact a teenager who, until last year, had no clue this hideous crap was playing out all over the world and, literally, right in front of my face?" Elias and Jake mirrored each other with a sharp intake of breath at my curtness.

"I heard a rumor… whisperings from the outcasts and less, well, involved members of The Collective about what it was that really made you different." Xander held my gaze again and I rolled my eyes. What was it with these guys, could no one answer a question in a direct fashion?

"For crying out loud, spit it out." The volume of my voice caused even me to jump a little. I was not known for losing my temper but this was one cryptic clue too far. "Just tell me, please."

"I think your gift is your ability to absorb powers." The silence from before befell the room once more and Celeste and Pierre couldn't pick their jaws up from the floor. The jigsaw pieces started to slide into place. He wanted me to try to control the girl. Could he be right? Was it possible? I knew better than to ask that question even in my head these days; everything was possible. Elias crept into my headspace.

You did start being able to do this when you met me. Coincidence? His voice faded out and I met his gaze as he shrugged his shoulders and suggested silently that it was a real possibility. I followed a dark urge that rose in my throat and closed my eyes. I pictured the girl and I felt the fuzz of possibility surge through my veins like I was channeling a current; my fingertips buzzed with promise of more power and I was made uneasy by the sensation that I wanted this a bit. What did that mean?

I kept my eyes firmly shut and lifted my arms until they rested across my chest. The room was silent but it broke with a contagious gasp, which my ears traced from person to person. I opened my right eye tentatively to see the girl stood across from me mirroring my pose; her arms crossed identically over her body. I couldn't trust it though; surely this was something that could have been staged? I proceeded to contort my shape into a series of fast, fluid movements to expose any attempt to trick me, but her body moved as though it were on invisible wires, connected to me on some molecular level. I was a puppet master and she was my marionette. It was the single most creepy and oddly exhilarating moment of my life. I stopped and she stopped, her head slumped as I paused to decide how to conclude this strange show and tell. I felt the connection wane in my mind as I distanced myself and allowed the image of her behind my closed eyes to fade. When I looked back at her she was roused, looking nothing more than a little dazed and smirked at me with much more of 'we told you so' look than you would expect for someone so susceptible to mind control. If I was to turn into the kind of megalomaniac that tends to hunt me then there really could be trouble.

I stumbled and almost fell into the chair at the huge desk and no sooner had I landed than Jake was next to me; his face ashen and not like normally when he was worried, he looked scared, of me. My heart started to race and any slight odd enjoyment dissipated at the look in his eyes, it was like he didn't recognize me at all. Something in my soul burned and I knew I had to focus, to stay me. If he was scared of me and didn't like this side of who I am I was in very real danger of losing him, and The Collective and the rest of these guys had no idea how dangerous it was to show me anything that would push him away.

COLLECTOR

I shooed everyone but Jake and Xander out of the room; the audience was getting too much and I was feeling more than a little self-conscious. I quizzed Xander about his companions and their gifts, some I had already experienced in the catacombs and others that were new. There were just two others that would be useful and he brought them back into me like lab rats. The whole being revered thing wasn't getting any easier and I had to bite my lip to stop myself yelling at them to stop looking at me.

The first was Jude. He couldn't have been more than seventeen, with olive skin, dark hair and a lilt of a Spanish accent. He reminded me of Elias with a tan but he didn't have the swagger to go with it. His eyes could barely fix on one spot, let alone on me and his hands were wringing through and through each other. I had a flashback to not so long ago when that was me: shy, terrified, out of depth. So, not that much was different on those scores, just that I was better at hiding it – that and the fact that if I acted scared I would not only bring about my own demise but probably that of, now, hundreds of people. Excellent, no pressure.

"Jude can, well, show her, Jude." Xander stepped to one side and let the young man stand alongside him. Jude placed on the table a small, delicate hand mirror that I recognized from the upstairs bathroom. He put an outstretched hand above it, no more than three inches and closed his eyes. Jake and I exchanged bemused glances but if anything, we had learned that there was no point in guessing anymore, our imaginations could barely begin to comprehend the depths of mystery and the number of things we didn't previously understand or know existed in this world.

The mirror rattled ever so lightly on the table, rocking on its gilt edges for a few seconds before hairline cracks spread like an icy web across its face and it exploded into thousands of shards. Jake and Xander shielded their eyes but just like I had done in France, I raised a protective hand and froze the flying glass in mid-air. I lowered my hand and the tiny, glitter–like fragments floated slowly to the table top.

"So what is this, your thing? I mean, I don't get it?" Jude looked crestfallen and Xander put a reassuring hand on his shoulder. "I'm sorry, I wasn't trying to be rude. I just don't know what I am seeing and what these things mean anymore. I have been on a pretty steep learning curve... I mean, a year ago my biggest worry was if I had the right books in my book bag or if I should tie my hair up or not... this stuff, well, I am trying so hard to take it in my stride but it is getting really hard."

The awkwardness of my rant hung between us all. Jude sat down and beckoned for me to do the same. He put my hand in his and I felt it instantly; constant, tiny vibrations. I looked at him, puzzled.

"It's kind of energy control... I can cause glass to break, walls to fall or earth to move." He smirked and was more like Elias than I realized. Jake tensed and shot him a look. He still had my hand in his. "You try." His grip tightened momentarily and the familiar rush passed over me, his ability flowing through me, adding to my own ever-growing repertoire of sideshow abilities.

I looked around me, unsure of what to try it on. Xander rose to his feet and slid a glass tumbler over to me. I pushed it further away so if it works none of us would be hit by the shrapnel and I started to concentrate as hard as I could. It was getting more difficult now though, defining which gift I wanted to take out and when. My mind had become a lending library of strange skills and the unknown. I was rifling through my own head to find the thing I wanted. I stared at the glass, my hand outstretched, and increasingly sweaty palm facing the side of it. I focused until my head burned with concentration. The swoosh of the glass sliding at speed along and then off the table caught us all by surprise by virtue of the fact we were waiting for a smash. Wrong gift.

"It is ok. Try again." I appreciated that Jude was trying to be encouraging, but it came off as patronizing and I didn't like it. I stomped moodily to the end of the table and put the glass back on the spot from before. I wasn't good at not being good at things, even if the thing in question was some superpower I had never known existed until moments before.

My hand tingled and twitched and I fought the urge to smash the glass with my fist instead. It rumbled and shifted on the spot for what seemed like an eternity before exploding into a million glittering shards. As quick as my right hand had caused the chaos my left hand, without my awareness of a prompt, shot out and had already tamed the haze of shimmering daggers to a hovering swarm that fell with a wind-chime like tinkle to the table.

"Errmm... WOW." Jake was opened mouthed and Xander and Jude were silenced too. I had never managed to combine gifts before and while I could hardly take credit, it wasn't like I meant to, I had still done it and this was a good step. Gaining control was important, for winning.

I felt odd, like I had simultaneously started to find some answers and discover more questions at the same time. We had come all this way, sacrificed so much with some crazy notion that Jean would be able to help me with his expertise and instead it seemed fate had something altogether more obscure planned. How the two were interlinked was beyond me, but if nothing else, I was accustomed now to feeling perpetually confused. Then there was Alice, what about her? I certainly had some kind of duty to release her from the hell they must have had her in for so long.

Jude's slow clapping was what brought me round from the runaway mine train of my thoughts. He and Xander were exchanging smug glances; they never doubted me.

"So, is there more or are we done?" I directed my question at Xander, he seemed most attuned to us maximizing the opportunity. I was wary of coming across as pleased with myself or seeming to convey too much confidence at this point; the mounting pressure of so many people's hopes and aspirations for me was becoming a pressure almost too much to bear.

He glanced at Jude and nodded silently. Jude proceeded to disappear into the kitchen. Silence hung between us in his absence and Jake pulled me into him, arms wrapped around me tightly. No one spoke, which was something that was growing increasingly common. I suppose there was no handbook for polite chit-chat in some situations.

I closed my eyes to aid thinking or just to find peace for a moment but the second that sliver of light disappeared beneath my eyelids, she was there: Alice.

I spoke silently, channeling every synapse and tiny feeling I felt when I communicated with Elias this way. *Where. Are.You?* At first, nothing. Her head hung limp in the darkness and for a split second the grey of her skin made me believe it might already have been too late. But, her bare feet twitched beneath her where they lay crossed under her seat. Her head lifted, she was weaker still.

Her dry lips were bleeding and chapped from malnutrition and dehydration, she looked like she was already dead. Maybe she was. They would only give her the most essential amount of sustenance to keep her alive, compliant but never strong enough to be a threat, to leave them with no road map to me and my powers.

Her mouth opened and she winced in agony with the movement. Then her voice, a whisper travelled to me on an exhausted breath. How long could she fight like this? Why hadn't she just given up and left them without help?

Then, three words which I may have already on some level known but been forced for sanity's sake to ignore: *Coming for you.* With that the darkness fell like a curtain in a theatre for the macabre and she was gone. Warning - that was the only card she had left. She had no other sense of purpose but to feel like she gave me the best possible chance. Chance to do what though? Run? Fight? Destroy them?

Jude swung the door open and appeared in the room with a petite, dark-haired girl who looked somewhere lost between terrified and confused. I wasn't sure if was just my heightened sense of awareness because of all the new 'stuff' I could do, but in the silence, I was sure I could hear her heart beating in her chest, the blood coursing through her veins like a torrent of water through a tunnel too narrow. She was uneasy; I think she thought she was like some kind of sacrificial offering. She was afraid, of me. The hummingbird beat of her heart was distracting and the sound flooded my head. I was brought back to the room by the snap of Jude's fingers just inches from my face, "Shall we?" I nodded silently, flashing the briefest of smiles in the direction of the dark-haired girl whose name I didn't yet know; a likely fruitless attempt to ease her concerns. What was I to her? A freak? A legend? A real witch, the kind to fear?

Xander shunted her forward so she took center stage of our group, her arms wrapped themselves around her tiny frame and suddenly she looked so young and I wanted just to tell her to run, to escape this madness before she became too embroiled to ever recover from what she saw or learned in that room.

She didn't even say a word; she just closed her eyes and started to hum a low reverberating sound which I felt deep within the pit of my stomach. Jake and Elias looked first to each other, then to me; a sensation and an unspoken awareness that there was something big coming. The hum grew to a rumble, which in turn became a thunderous roar and the air was moving too. It felt like what I imagined standing in the wake of a jumbo jet engine would be like. My insides were vibrating and the sensation was making me dizzy. I saw Xander retreat through the door backwards, closely followed by Jude and then we fell.

When we came round we were sprawled out in various positions across the room. Jake was holding a cold compress to an angry looking bump which glowed from beneath his palm. Elias was suspiciously eyeing the girl who was speaking quickly and somewhat emotionally to a reassuring Jude.

"OK. What was that one?" I was slightly perturbed by the fact my curiosity and desire to master this particular gift was overshadowing all else. I knew I should have been worried about Jake, getting pissed at Elias for stirring or feeling anxious, but my fingertips were tingling with anticipation. The thrill of all of this was starting to burst through the twisting fear in my gut and that had to be a good thing. I knew my endless battle with the darkness and my own anxiety was my greatest weakness and their easiest way in.

There were no prizes for assuming I could absorb hers too. I could and it felt even better than I imagined. Naturally there were less takers the second time around;

unsurprisingly, not many of the gang were prepared to be sent into a temporary coma by a sound so all-consuming it made you fear your eyes might explode from your head while your legs gave way beneath you. It was a heady if not disturbing combination.

EXODUS

We didn't talk so much about the day, despite how eventful it had been. Jake knew well enough that there was too much in my head to try to unlock it in one pre-bed conversation. He opted wisely for just holding me instead and I backed into his arms, willing sleep to envelop me.

It wasn't meant to be. Sleep it seemed was impossible, it was all I could do to lay there and hope it got better, soon. Jake's protective hand draped over my collar bone. His rhythmic breathing should have lulled me into slumber but it felt more like a ticking clock, counting the seconds until some unknown finale. I knew only that I was aware of something building, a seismic change in the air around me and I felt like Alice was closer. It could have just been residual tension but I was fully aware by now that these feelings usually meant something.

I headed downstairs to grab a drink, maybe break something and see if I could put it back together with my mind, you know, the usual stuff. The house was silent and almost pitch black but as I reached the ground floor I could see an arrow of light shooting across the floor from the kitchen door which lay ajar. I pulled it open cautiously not expecting anyone else to be up at such an ungodly hour.

The door made a sweeping sound as it opened which startled whoever was looking in the refrigerator into letting out a high pitched yelp, followed by a series of foreign words which I could only presume were curse words, judging by the tone.

Xander appeared, pale faced with his hands full of snacks and some juice boxes. He looked guilty and panicked to have been caught out.

"Did I miss out on an invitation for midnight snacks?" I smiled but he didn't click and was still staring half shocked like a kid caught out by its parents. "Relax. I'm kidding. But, what are you doing? Don't you sleep?"

"You're awake… I could ask you the same."

"Well, you could, but I am not the one with armfuls of cold meat in a kitchen that isn't mine in the middle of the night." He looked down at his hands and smiled.

"Fair point. Look, I'm sorry. Please, sit." He placed his stash down on the counter top and pulled out a stool at the breakfast bar. "I needed a few supplies for the road."

"You're leaving? But we... today was only..." I felt a strange surge of panic despite the fact these people hadn't been in my life twenty four hours earlier. I guessed it stemmed from having more people around that were like me. I had felt so lonely lately and having a name for what I could do, belonging to a group of people not just people in history, but real live people who believed me, understood me, that was a greater comfort than I had realized. Now it was on the brink of being ripped away, it suddenly felt more important. Isn't that always the way though?

"We must. We never intended to stay but when it was clear how, attached, you were feeling to us..." I shot him a 'what the hell?' glance, "I sensed it the minute we finished up tonight. I don't blame you. You must feel very alone." Was he reading my mind? "But, it only makes you and us more vulnerable. The more people you care about, the more they will use it against you. So now you know, now you have seen and felt what we can do and you can do it for yourself, we must go. Tonight." He started putting the food into a waiting bag, his eyes on a level with the counter the whole time.

"I guess that makes sense but I, I don't feel ready." I felt a wave of confession about to swell in my stomach. Words I had tried to bury so deep, thoughts I had denied for so long started to fight their way out of me. "You have helped me, really. But as well as that, you have shown me how much there is to learn. By putting it into perspective how powerful I might be, you have shown me how far I need to go and I am living under this ticking time bomb of a clock. Every second of my life I panic that I am wasting it, not pushing myself enough but the truth is I am too scared to do exactly that. I am scared of finding out how powerful I am in case it isn't enough, or worse, in case it is so much stronger than I realize and I don't want to let something out that I can never take back." I shook away the other words that hung on my tongue. "Anyway. This isn't your problem. I, I'm sorry. Just forget it. I understand why you need to leave and I am grateful you came at all. I guess I just want to learn how to keep my humanity in all of this." Xander's face had softened through my confession.

"Your humanity is a choice. You won't lose it if you choose to keep it. You love Jake fiercely; well, use that, use it as your anchor and allow it to bring you back to him. Everything from here on out is choices. It might feel like everything is foretold, but none of us ever knew the end of the story, you're writing it, so choose your words carefully and create something you can look back on and feel ok with."

"Thank you." He nodded as a wise, knowing smile spread across his face. He swung the bag over his shoulder and walked by me to leave. He paused as he reached me, towering over my seated frame and gently kissed the top of my head.

"We believe in you. Really." And with that he left me in the false light and silence. I had lost my desire to drink and to practice, I clung to his words about Jake and I crept upstairs and into the warm hollow of his arms and chest. He stirred slightly but settled as I watched him drift away.

The dawn light was starting to illuminate the room in a soft glow. Jake turned over in his sleep and left me free to silently maneuver out of the bed. I reached the door when I heard the familiar but feint sound of the gates of the house coming to a stop. No-one should be coming or going at this time. Then I remembered, Xander. I glanced at the clock on the landing from my frozen spot in the doorway; just five thirty. My heart pulsed, accelerating above the only other noise of Jake's breathing. I padded back to the other side of the room and slowly and discreetly as possible I moved back the tiniest section of the curtains so as not to draw attention to myself in the increasing light.

Xander, Jude, the dark haired coma-inducing girl and all of their companions filed nervously out of the gate and piled into a waiting van. Xander ushered them all along, signaling for silence three or four times before hopping in himself. He reached to slide the door to a close and just as the space shut his eyes locked on mine for a moment. He paused and offered nothing more than a nod. It was a goodbye and a good luck. They had served their purpose;

sharing their gifts and, perhaps, the promise of ensuring the 'prophecies' were real was the main idea behind coming out to find me. They had done that and now they wanted to be as far away as possible. I was relieved that it was nothing more sinister, as noises in the night these days could be anything but I hoped to whatever deity was awake with me at that hour that they at least left with hope, but mostly that it wasn't misplaced in me.

I didn't bother going back to bed, it hardly seemed worth it. Instead I holed myself up in the dining room-cum-library, where I practically main-lined coffee and practiced my new skills as best I could without an assistant. After ditching revision last night I was playing catch up. By the time Jake and Pierre surfaced almost in sync at nine, I had made some great progress.

I opened the day's conversation with my early morning discovery that our guests had unexpectedly left. The guys didn't seemed too shocked, or to really give a crap at all. It was less baggage as far as they were concerned. It was weird to have had such fleeting but significant guests, that you could share so much with people in a limited time. I shouldn't really have been shocked that no-one else cared as much as me because, when it came down to it, everyone still just thought it was me and me alone that would do it, fix it.

It took about an hour of coffee and weirdly complacent chatter before anyone noticed he was gone. Elias hadn't come down and he was normally the first; being as complex as him did not lend itself to long, relaxing lie-ins.

The guys shrugged it off and were willing to dismiss it as part of Elias's increasingly anti-social behavior, but I knew better. Rightly or wrongly he was invested in this mess. I spoke to him silently, urged him to let me know what he was up to. The line stayed eerily quiet for too long. He was actively blocking me out. Unacceptable to say the least, this wasn't the time for lone missions and misplaced heroism. Though it was fairly commonplace for him to decide his own path and think 'to hell with the rest of us'.

Elias, where the hell are you? Jake was watching me intently; I think without powers of his own his feelings for me attuned his senses to mine. When I was distracted and distant, the way I had to be to speak with Elias, he always ended up just flashing furtive glances my way, or if he was really pissed, just staring straight at me the whole time. This occasion was the former which was somehow worse.

The silence was deafening. *Elias, come on, cut the crap.* I couldn't have been clearer if I tried. I was throwing everything at it but it was like trying to tune into a radio that wasn't plugged in. I was getting increasingly frustrated and my repeated 'head-desking' was attracting attention.

Just as I was about to totally lose it, he faltered, he seemingly unintentionally let me through and it didn't even feel like he had noticed, which meant I was getting better at this thing. Point to me. He was cursing, and he was on edge. Then I felt panic, not mine but his. It engulfed me and flooded my senses to the point my vision went dull and the light started to dim. His heart was racing and he was cursing because he was struggling, fighting.

Don't come in Scarlett. It's what they want. Don't do this. Don't give them the satisfaction. His voice rasped in a dry throat and he heaved against some unknown force. I let the connection drop, more in horror than with intention. There was only one 'they' we spoke of these days. My behavior had roused the interest of the room and they looked to me for some explanation but at that moment my hands were shaking uncontrollably and that look of disgust on Jake's face morphed to match my own; they knew it was bad.

"They have him. Elias. He is with them." My head fell into my waiting hands on the table top. I felt the unwelcome rise of a lump in my throat as I fought to work out how, why and what for? They know about Jake, they didn't try to take him, or attempt to come here for me which could only mean something worse was coming. Elias was secondary to them, so why now?

It simply didn't make sense, how had they got to him here? Why would he willingly go to them? I shoved my previous mistrust and memories of the sketchy video recordings from Paris to the back of my mind; I knew him better than that now. If they had managed to get that close, why couldn't I tell? Every step forward there were ten back. Then like a bolt of lightning, it made perfect sense. Ava. The only reasons he would throw himself so carelessly into their path is if he thought, or knew, they had her or she was at risk, or perhaps if they had me.

Without any cruel intention, I blocked out the room; the people stood fixated on my face waiting eagerly for me to share my plan, some detail. I had to focus and it had to be just me. I phased out their glances, the dull sounds that forced their way through the tall windows from the normal world beyond and I focused on the newer parts of myself. The darker, somehow smarter and more calculated version of Scarlett. I felt a pang of shame that I was almost silently celebrating these changes, willing more of them to occur. It had become challenging to think of the person I was, the innocence I had retained now lost to a world where it seemed reasonable and necessary to open my mind to the possibility of hurting people even if it was for the good of the rest of the world. I knew I was lost but I had little choice but to continue on the path that had seemingly laid in wait for me my whole life. My conscience twitched feverishly in my head, reminding me not to lose sight, not to lose who I was.

I may have had to encounter terrible things, behave in ways I would never have imagined, but I prayed I would come out of this in the knowledge that I acted at all times in good faith and that I had to remember no matter what they did that I was better, I was a good person and how passionately I didn't ever, ever want to be like them. Power is intoxicating but it is no more than an alluring fallacy, it means nothing, knows nothing of love, of giving, it is selfish and consuming and I wouldn't be like them. I needed to harness the power but never succumb to it. I shook off the lingering reminders of how much of a rush it felt to collect the powers from The Collective, how full of purpose it made me feel. I had to stay focused. My entire life felt like it was hanging in the balance and I wanted so badly to have all the answers right there, be totally confident in the good guys winning, but The Venari and their Sanguinary friends seemed always to be ahead; ironic given I am the one with the power of premonition.

I had barely acknowledged my feet carrying me from the room. I took the stairs two by two and locked myself in the sanctuary of the first floor main bathroom. It was a light, huge space with a free standing bath and enough room for a chaise longue and separate cubicle housing the most grand and complex looking shower I had ever seen. As I slid down the back of the locked door I was relieved at the lack of any following footsteps, our little group was so important to me, Jake the most, but it was claustrophobic too; expectant eyes on me the whole time filled with such hope.

My options were to get back in touch with Elias and risk them doing God knows what to him to find out what I was doing and where I was, or contact Alice. I hated to think of her safety in such throwaway terms but if they were busy with him, chances were she was off the proverbial hook for a while and was my best hope.

In the past she was the initiator, she found me so it had come to the time the textbook of hocus pocus that was now my brain had to be studied and I needed to pull some of this so-called skill out of the bag when it actually mattered.

Crossed legged and with eyes closed, I searched for her triggers in my brain, recalled the sensation that ran through me when she came through in my dreams. The inside of my head was like a swirling vortex of information and complex synapses to every available end, all the wiring was there, the challenge came in connecting them together.

The chaos felt tidal, every time I thought I had found the path the wave of certainty moved out of reach and I lost her. I drew in a deep, pensive breath fighting off the exhaustion; this should be simple task to bring on.

"Come on. Please." My fists were balled tight and I was losing patience when, suddenly, I felt her. The page was still blank in my mind but there was a swift, inexplicable chill that spread through me and I knew it was her. It turned out that rewinding your mind and thought process wasn't impossible but, wow, it was taxing. I trawled back, as focused as I could be on her and there was that feeling again.

Alice, is this you? Can you feel me, hear me? For a moment there was just silence, but shortly I could physically feel her pushing through, it was hurting her and I could sense the energy seeping from her broken body but I was grateful to her for hanging on. I had been so sure her fight was over when we had been on our way to Amsterdam and I learned of her survival, so to still be trying now was braver than anything I was doing.

She didn't respond immediately and the silence started to bore holes in my concentration; it gets hard to hold onto nothing. Then, the faintest of sounds broke through and she was with me.

Alice, I... I found myself engulfed in emotion for all I knew that she had lost for me, to fight to help me, a person she didn't know and was possible she would never get the chance to meet. I felt the ethereal reach out of her hand.

Don't. I could hear her clearly for the first time, though the vision of her was still really hard to make out. *Don't be sorry. I don't want that.* Her voice broke as her words rasped through a weak, dry throat. The connection faltered. *I just want to know it wasn't for nothing, that you won't give up?*

Tears pooled in my eyes and I felt the familiar tug of emotion in my aching throat; a translation of the guilt for my own self-pity when she was there for trying to help me and I dared to feel hard done to.

I'm not, I promise. I have been working on my powers, realizing my potential. It is getting better but I don't think I have much time left.

You're right. There isn't much time. They know where you are. I froze and my heart's thump dulled to what felt like a complete stop in my throat. *They won't come, not yet. They want to discuss their own plans first but you need to be ready, soon.*

How... was it Elias? Did he tell them?

This is your friend. The one I sense here? No. He hasn't talked and they have tried hard to make him but they are putting all they can behind this. You are their biggest ever investment and they want to cash it in, they won't stop now.

The light was fading with my quickening pulse and all I could feel and see was the force of her efforts, her sheer will to show me something. Words had gone and in their place a distant, static, blurred image. The connection waned and I grasped frantically at the image she was trying to show me, only to catch the very briefest and undefined of images. I had no idea what I was seeing; a symbol? A logo? Perhaps a structure? It was geometric and angular, but there were curves too; the line was almost gone and so weak it was too fuzzy to focus any further. A primal growl of frustration left my throat. Why, with all this power I could harness, was something as simple as photo-shopping an image with my mind so taxing and nigh on impossible?

I came around and knocked my head back in frustration. Pen and paper, I needed to draw it before it was lost for good. I stumbled from room to room emptying drawers and clearing shelves before I found myself in the room I shared with Jake. I clutched at the discarded receipts that lay among foreign coins and took the nearest pen I could find, which ended up being my eyeliner, and set it to work.

I closed my eyes again to allow my brain direct contact with my hands, no distractions. I scrawled and sketched blindly and what started as desperate, staccato movements became more fluid as my hands followed my brain's instruction.

When I ran out of momentum, I opened my eyes and found something clearer than I had expected but no more helpful. I gripped the paper and took the stairs two at a time.

By the time I re-joined the group, I was breathless and clammy from my exertions and communing with the almost dead.

"Jean... turn on the screens, I need to put something up there, you know, try the whole projection thing." He nodded in silence and quickly set about illuminating the wall.

"If I do that can you somehow use what I show you to search for it?"

"Like through the web? Sure... it may take me a few minutes but I can run it through some software and search." He had quickly become one of my favorite people. He was efficient, articulate and endlessly intelligent but he didn't ask too many questions, just got the job done.

Jake shifted behind me and the others sat, still silent, it

felt for the first time that they too knew when it wasn't the right time to be asking questions. The balance of power was changing and it was starting to feel a little more them and me, but I knew it really came down to the fact that we were heading into the final showdown and they were rightly scared and feeling helpless. I empathized while trying to remain composed.

Jean shot me a nod when he was ready for me and I pulled up a chair in front of the screens the way I had been in that medical cave in Paris. I closed my eyes and pushed the image I drew outward from my mind. The paper was still screwed up in my hand and I used it, feeding from it to project the image onto the screens. They flashed and flickered blue, then gray, then white. The outline of the image appeared and then disappeared while I fought to concentrate hard enough.

A faint 'woah' from Celeste behind me was all the indication I needed that something was working. I opened my eyes slowly, desperate to see but not break the connection and there was the shape. It was definitely a structure of some kind. It looked weirdly like a spaceship but even for this crazy scenario that would be a step too far.

Jean was tapping away frantically on his keyboard next to me and the internet browser sprang to life in one of the currently redundant screens alongside my creation. "Ok, Scarlett, got it." I immediately exhaled the tension from my lungs and miraculously the picture hung there, suspended on the screens without even faltering. He clicked away for what felt like ages and then, like magic, the image search spread across the sea of glass and showed us what it was in glorious, three-foot technicolor.

"The European Parliament in Strasbourg. What the hell do you want with that place, Scarlett?" Jean looked at me puzzled as he tapped through a series of images: different perspectives, views of sprawling rooms equipped to host world leaders or greedy, masochistic megalomaniacs from around the globe.

"That's it. That is where they are taking him, Elias, and where they are waiting for me." Silence remained, their minds ticking over. "It is perfect for them. A home for the great and the good, high security, zero risk and no-one blinks at an influx of powerful people coming together. They expect me to chase Elias to that place."

"That sounds like you have no intention of such a thing?" Celeste's voice was testy, like she was passing judgment on me.

"Look, I want him back, of course I do, but I doubt very much that heading to Strasbourg sans plan and all guns blazing is going to end in any other way than with all of us imprisoned or worse. Whatever the move, it has to be considered. This is what all this preparation has been for, to lead me to them and I have to be sure that when I get there in front of them that I can win. I either end it or it ends me."

EGO

Her face fell. "We cannot leave him there with those monsters. Who knows what they will do to him to draw you out." Nothing like laying on the guilt.

"Celeste," she jumped at my tone, "no-one knows more than me the risks here, or what they are capable of and I am sorry that Elias is there and I will be doing everything I can to get him out, but right now I have to trust that he can look after himself and that he will understand my reluctance to simply show up. Do you want to die?" Silence. "Well, do you? I mean, they will not hesitate and they will be creative. The Sanguinaries are like a living nightmare; they are pretty much bred for the purpose of making little problems like us fade away and disappear. I am willing to bet that our friends in Paris were the tame version, but their strength, their size versus us? So, we can choose to wait and let me figure this thing out or we can go and become their play things. It's up to you."

Still stunned by my increasingly terse tone, she backed off physically into her chair and threw her hands into the air in reluctant concession. Pierre looked on, arms folded, he was weighed down with sadness for Elias and I could sense how alone he felt without him. We were the new kids to him, Elias was his safety blanket, even if he was a pain ninety nine per cent of the time.

"I need to do some reading, more research and I need to make sure certain things are in order before we go." Jake let out a nervous laugh.

"Sounded like you were talking about preparing a will or something." He searched my face for some reassurance and I couldn't offer any.

"No, not a will as such. But there are a few things I need to take care of in relation to Mom and well, you know, planning. In case."

"In case of what? You can't seriously be saying what I think you're saying?!" His hands clasped my shoulders and he tried to shake whatever stupidity he thought I was blighted with of out me. He was scared. So was I. But I knew of all things I couldn't walk into their path again without at least saying some of the things I may never get a chance to in the real world.

My mind flashed to Lydia and Taylor, the friends that had so admirably stood by me without ever even understanding what it was I was involved in. I could easily imagine their summer, the polar opposite to my own in every way I was sure. There would be nail painting, mall visits, boy-related carb and sugar overdoses and cheesy movies together before college. Then there was Mom; I had feelers out, I knew she was still safe as it stood, but whatever was going on, she was still alone and my half-baked 'I'm doing great' texts were unlikely to work forever. I wanted to know, to be sure that I would be there with her again, able to bury my head into her shoulder and cry tears of relief that this was over, but I knew it wasn't a bet many people would take.

"I'm just saying it cannot hurt to enter this situation with a little realism. I don't know whether what I know is enough. All I can do is hope and, with that in mind, I need to take stock of a few things and make sure if this doesn't work my way that I have done what I needed to."

He shook his head, unable to process the scale of what I was saying. I didn't say it lightly and I certainly was going to do everything in my power to avoid it coming to any of this, but I was done with speculation and dreaming, I was facing the facts and acting the only way I could see was right. He stormed out of the room and we each listened as he took the stairs two at a time.

I left behind him, still buzzing with unspoken thoughts and theories about my behavior, my thought process and what I 'should' be feeling, saying and doing in this situation. I wanted to run after Jake and be enveloped in his arms, but I had to focus and the strain of his struggle was putting more pressure on me and my ability to concentrate waned every time I looked at him and saw how hard he was taking all of this. Though leaving him to suffer in fear went against every single instinct I had. It was torture.

I tip-toed up the stairs and moved swiftly and quietly beyond the closed door of the bedroom we shared. I entered a small study I had noticed before but had not been inside and I found myself sitting at the desk. I picked up a pen and some paper and found words fell from my mind, words I hadn't really allowed to form fully. It was an instinctive process.

I started with Mom. She was at the fore of my mind at the moment I sat down and all feeling pertaining to her just fell out of me.

Mom,

I am not sure entirely what it means to be writing this. Maybe it is over and we can look at this together, or maybe the worst has already happened but, for all our trials and tribulations, we have made it through so much and I will never be able to really articulate what your constant love and support have meant to me.

I know you think I can be selfish and perhaps you are right, but I love you so much and there is nothing that can ever change that. Even if I am not there to tell you every day, believe I am doing it in some other way. Always.

You showed me what strength is, what it means to take the best kind of chances, to offer yourself up to someone you love and sacrifice what you want for the good of others. This past year has been tough and I know you have so many questions for me. You deserve the answers, no matter how hard they may be for you to hear. What happened with Jake's dad was more, well, complicated than I ever told you and I am so sorry now that I am having to write this and share it with you this way. You deserve better and I don't want you to blame anything that has happened on you. You couldn't have stopped any of this, it is bigger than us. Older and more powerful.

The answers are so many and so vast that I can't even write it all here. Everything you need to know is already waiting for you at the house. There is a loose floorboard beneath my bed. Read my notes, read the papers and you'll see why I have had to be so secretive and how I was only ever trying to protect you.

I know you always said you hated me getting so grown up because it felt like I needed you less, but I promise it feels completely the opposite. I have never felt like I needed you more.

I love you. S xxxxx

The final kiss was blotted by a tear that I wasn't planning on shedding. I was trying in vain to detach myself from what I was doing but the pain of keeping it all in was dizzying my mind. The taste of salt flooded my mouth as more tears fell and I brushed my lips with my tongue to keep them from the paper below.

I wrote matching letters, though littered each with their own personal relevance to my dad, Brooke and then worst of all, Jake. His was the hardest.

Dearest Jake,

I don't even know how I can ever thank you. You turned what felt like the scariest and most vulnerable part of my life into something incredible and beautiful. Meeting you changed me, changed my life and all for the better. I couldn't have imagined finding you or a love like we have. We are the people I read about and I had no idea how amazing life could be until I had you. I know it's real because we never got the chance to just be, to be in love... the shadows hung over us from the very beginning but we always managed to make something amazing come from it.

You did the most incredible job in watching over me, no matter what you think, what you feel now reading this; I want you to know, to understand, you did it all right. This is not on you. You saved me the minute we met without even realizing. That first day, outside the hall, I knew then I would have you in my life, that I would need you. I felt it.

When I close my eyes you are what I see, you and me

and those fairy lights in that lock-up, the fondue and the smell of your skin. You are my positive thoughts, Jake, and I can promise you that no matter what I walked into and how it ended, that you were my final thoughts, we were my final thoughts, because that is all that matters. For all my powers, you are the thing that makes me feel strongest.

If I can't be with you another second, I am already eternally grateful. I have known more joy even in our messed up time together than many people get in a lifetime and I want you to know that and remember it. You gave me a taste of life at its best.

I have so many memories that it is hard to pick one and of all the things I can think of, I don't know why I am stuck on this but I love the thought of you walking bare foot around the apartment, in those grubby gray sweats you never let me wash and the way you swig orange juice from the carton, which I should find gross and probably would if it were anyone else, but with you, I love it. I love all of you.

Please live. Read books, travel, breathe deeply and listen to amazing music. See places, meet people and know I will love you always.

S xxx

Writing something like that to him felt like the ink was mainlined from my heart; each word weakened me and for the first time I saw what they saw, the opportunity that he posed. He was my Achilles heel; they knew it and so did I and the worst part was facing the reality that no matter how much that was the case, I had to put everything else ahead of that even if it killed us both. The realization brought pure agony to the pit of my stomach and I heaved a huge breath to try to replenish my composure.

I carefully folded the delicate papers into matching envelopes and pressed them shut. I walked lightly through the silent house to Celeste's bedroom and pushed the pack of letters into the side pocket of her rucksack. She'd find them eventually and I knew I could trust her to make sure they found their way to the right people. She understood me more than perhaps many of the others in the party; she too had fought a battle between having the power to change her fate and the will or courage to do it. There was an unspoken synergy between us and I was sure it would be enough to endure whatever choices I made; to keep her faith in me when even those closest to me may struggle to understand.

I must have fallen asleep after I returned to sit, or hide at the desk, as I woke amidst fading light from the tiny rectangular window and the smell of yet more food from the kitchen downstairs. On the landing it was almost pitch black bar the diagonal strip of light that fanned out from beneath our closed bedroom door. Jake was clearly still holed up inside, while I hovered outside, listening for signs of life and my heart skipped when the light was broken by the movement of feet on the other side. I recognized the ridiculousness of hiding outside a room I shared with the guy I was in love with, but I couldn't bring myself to go in. My trembling hand hung millimeters from the handle on the broad wooden door but my head wouldn't let me connect the two. The light restored and the body owning the feet retreated; I exhaled the pent up breath that had been aching in my chest.

I took another pensive deep intake of air, a concession to the fact I knew I wasn't ready to go in there and face the conversation that was waiting on the other side of that door. I went downstairs to a quiet, distracted Jean. He knew I was coming to ask for help, he could feel the weight of my request already.

I walked into the kitchen; the lights blinding my exhausted eyes. I stared right at him, planning my request. His shoulders shot up, riddled with tension. "What does that look mean?"

I smirked, the poor guy had only been burdened with us for a matter of days but he knew the score well enough already. "I need to create some kind of distraction." He didn't relax yet, probably rightly so as what I was about to suggest was, at best, weak and, at worst, fatal.

"Go on."

"Well, I need to get closer to them without them realizing and I hoped somehow a combination of my powers and your technological know-how would be enough." His eyes had rolled so far back he looked almost dead.

"Get close… without them realizing? To the people who have another psychic, mystic or whatever the hell she is trained on you like a laser-guided missile… the one they have been torturing for years to find out all about you? Get close to those people in secret?"

I let out a deep sigh; when you put it like that it certainly sounded ridiculous, but I believed Alice was weak enough that I could send some dummy info her way so she wouldn't even be compromising herself; if she could say it like she meant it, they would believe it… she has always been right before and, as for Elias, he would rather die than give me up. It felt selfish and cruel to think that way but I had to find a way to get closer and I knew that their obsession with me didn't stop with Alice or Elias, they were investigating for themselves and if I could just leave a convincing enough breadcrumb trail to throw them off a little, I could divert some of the danger from my friends and sneak in through the back door to their little party, or whatever the hell it was, that was happening in Strasbourg.

"Look… I know what you think and I am pretty sure I agree. Its borderline insane, but look at what we are dealing with here; hardly your everyday dilemma, but I am pretty sure we can do this. If you and I can make it look like I went somewhere else even just for a day or two, we can make it work. Please."

We set about trying to make the best of my, apparently, fatally flawed plan. I spent some time in another one of the house's lesser used rooms practicing and harnessing the powers from our fleeting guests. It was exhilarating and I was oblivious to what anyone else was doing. Jake was still pissed at me and hadn't resurfaced since the bedroom sulking episode and I was, as expected, still wrangling with the weight of whether or not to speak to him or try to hold onto this new found resolve and be less of the old Scarlett. I didn't allow the long and worrisome internal monologue that so often dominated my life to even get started.

My resolve lasted through another two hours of practice until my head ached and my eyes burned. Powers were draining; they only made me feel powerful in the moment, afterward they left me hollowed out, vacant. Some of the new stuff was hard work, really serious. If my visions were the rookie stuff then these new powers were the masters of witchcraft: super complex, requiring insane levels of concentration and a strong constitution. I was feeling sick to my stomach through exertion.

I had grappled with the movement of objects, I had that now. I knew, and was terrified by, my ability to utilize the weird 'turn people's' brains off. I was torn by mind control; it felt so intrusive and abusive, such an invasion, but that was more when practicing, I knew I would feel differently if it was The Venari, not my friends, on the receiving end. My exhaustion was an enemy but I pushed through the pulsating ache in my brain. I felt shivers ripple through me as I projected my thoughts on to Jean's video wall. I saw

Mom and my heart ached. I couldn't really think too much of her because it sent me on too much of a rollercoaster. One minute it bolstered me for the fight, made me think of how I had to save her, but then that confidence would collapse and I would regress, engulfed by feelings of terror and desperate to crawl to her and be comforted. Knowing it wasn't an opportunity made it all even harder.

Jean was still downstairs working on the practical, as well as the technological elements, of the plan. I paid him a brief visit, told him to shelve it until the morning, we were both exhausted and the silence in the house only served to remind us both that this was the time normal humans were asleep. We shared a knowing nod goodnight on the landing at the top of the stairs. I stood still until I had watched him pass the threshold to his room.

I took a deep breath and pushed open the door to our bedroom. There was an almost imperceptible shuffle of bedclothes which was mostly masked by the door creaking to a stop, but it was unmistakable. The room was silent and Jake lay motionless in a mass of duvet, his head turned away to face the window; he was pretending to be asleep to avoid the conversation he knew we needed to have.

I wasn't exactly forthcoming myself; I meticulously brushed my teeth, combed my hair, arranged the toiletries in the bathroom and wiped down the sink and mirror before I realized there was nothing else to do but talk it out. Or fight it out.

I crawled reluctantly into bed beside him and was almost swayed into forgetting the issues, lulled into an almost stupor by his warmth and the real reasons why we fell out; his opinion that I was stupid for being willing to risk my life. If only he could see that it was really for everybody; for him above all. I can imagine a world where I have to give it all up, but only if I can continue to imagine the world fixed and with him still in it. That I could live with.

REALITIES

We exhaled at exactly the same time. He was listening for sure but his body was rigid, his response cold.

"I don't want to leave. I don't want to take this risk, but I have to."

"No, Scarlett, you don't... not alone at least."

"Jake. I am doing what I think is right and I need your support." He spun half way and faced the ceiling. I slid my hand across his chest.

"You want me to support your committing suicide? That's basically what you said downstairs, right?" his voiced was raised and my whole body tensed.

"That's not what this is…"

"You are so willing to leave me behind… again. I don't know what I am supposed to make of this, Scarlett. Maybe I am kidding myself, or you're kidding me and this, all we have, is not what I thought." His words were toxic and their effects…my skin crawled and I felt sick and hot. What was he suggesting?

"No. No. Jake. Please. How can you not know me?" He didn't move; his eyes were fixed on the ceiling. "This isn't about me caring less what happens to us, to me. It is about saving you. Saving everybody." Finally a thaw. He turned to face me, his eyes bewitched me instantly and I held back tears.

"Saving me?" His eyes were like mine… glassy and wide with fear.

"Yes, you. I love you more than I have ever loved anyone or anything. I can't do this if I think you might not come out the other side. That is what this is about… me loving you beyond the imaginable and wanting to keep you safe at all costs." I could feel the tension in his body ease under my hand as I spoke.

His face moved within inches of mine and the warmth of his breath teased my face, which went cold where tears had coursed down my cheeks. His lips found mine and in a slow, silent way he showed me he understood.

I cried as we kissed, frightened, panicked tears which were less than the tip of the iceberg. I thought I had known fear in Salem, and again in Paris, but I knew that what was coming was different, darker and more likely to end badly than anything else we had been through so far. We talked and kissed it out for what felt like hours; the air between us heavy with fear and a combination of strong emotions we struggled to articulate. When Jake's breathing finally labored, his head resting in my arms, I just lay there with my thoughts and a pounding of adrenalin infused fear beating within my chest.

I heard footsteps lightly padding along the hall outside. I thought we were all in bed already, but it was no surprise that everyone was a little unsettled. Celeste had been prone to nightmares since Paris and she often got up for some air to clear her head.

I knew it was just a few hours before the ball really started rolling and I would have to make plans, leave them all behind. Even after our discussion this evening, I wasn't sure how that would work. I knew Jake wouldn't't let me simply walk out the door. As he slept, I tried to play out as many of the scenarios as I could imagine and I was actually surprised at how many ways I could think of, but none of them ended well.

When I finally slept, I dreamt all night of Alice and Elias, of the outcome of what felt sometimes like a totally pointless crusade. The crescendo of this ongoing nightmare was upon me and, despite knowing it was coming, had been coming for so long, it didn't ease the confusion. I wanted so badly to end it and when I got it right, really tapped into my anger, I felt ok, better than ok, I felt confident and powerful and I liked it. But, when I let that dark knot in my stomach turn or the doubt that I spent my life trying to bury at the back of my mind escape just a tiny bit, the walls came crashing down and the well of vulnerability overflowed into my bloodstream and sucked the strength from me. I had to learn to control the fear and the doubt or it was going to get me, and possibly others, killed.

When the light filtered in and broke me from a poor attempt at sleep, my aching body instinctively reached for Jake. Eyes still closed, my arms searched for him, but where I should have found his warmth there was just a void. My eyes, suddenly more than awake flashed open, the sheets were cold and the house was silent. I already knew what had happened but I refused to acknowledge it, determined to examine every single other possibility no matter how vain the hope appeared to be.

I ran down the stairs and swept through the rooms that had played host to plans and discussions and heated disagreements about how to untangle ourselves from this mess and I found myself at Jean's desk. On it lay a huge doodle of what I had seen, the building, the venue for what was about to happen. I stared at it, fighting it, but the realization I was so busy denying was working its way to the front of my mind. I ran to the bathroom where the porcelain felt shockingly cool beneath my sweating palms. Huge dry heaves wracked my body and I spluttered my way through them before collapsing on the floor. I knew why the bed was empty, why it was cold and the pain of the reality smashed through my core like I had been hit by a truck.

I hadn't had all the time I had expected, the plans had barely been discussed. I wrote down my thoughts, a breadcrumb trail for Jean to leave, positioning me elsewhere... strange occurrences, fake tickets purchased in my name then a few apologetic question marks for where I hoped he would have some ideas. I scraped my belongings from the dresser in the bedroom. Passport, photos of Mom, Dad and Brooke, loose change and a handful of notes and the bracelet Jake had given me. I thought of the letters I had prepared and toyed with retrieving them, denying that there was any reason for them to exist, but I knew, if ever there was a time I might need them to be ready for distribution, it was now. Just in case. I put the bracelet on my wrist and fiddled with it nervously as I stood and surveyed what I had laid out.

I latched the door behind me and slid silently through the front gates. I stopped just past where the narrow road twisted and obscured the view of the house and every fiber of my body told me to run back inside and lock the door; not to face what was happening but I pushed my legs forward and kept walking. I kept up a strong pace and found myself looking behind every few seconds pumped with adrenalin and paranoia about who or what may be behind me. I saw a large man dressed all in black and despite the dim morning light he wore sunglasses; my back tensed as we passed on the deserted street and all I could imagine was him turning on me, doubling back and grabbing me. A few moments later and it was clear he was not in fact a Sanguinary, but he, and more than a handful of others, would raise my concern on this leg of my journey.

I managed to negotiate the streets and used a small map I found in Jean's library to navigate my way to the bus terminal.

I picked a seat right at the back, seemed sensible to have the view of every other passenger as the ride to the train station was long enough that I needed to keep my guard up. One of my three cheap European cells vibrated in my pocket. It was Jean. He had woken and was on the case.

I wish you hadn't gone alone, but I know how you feel about this. I am going to do all I can. Right now you appear to the rest of the world to be heading back to Paris. I'll keep it that way as long as possible. Stay quiet, move fast and pay cash. Also, destroy this phone and use the new sim card I gave you. I assume Jake is with you, tell him the same. Be safe.

I texted my thanks, ignoring the rest of his requests and

fell back into my seat. Just the sight of his name made my heart ache. I don't know how much of a head start he had and I didn't dare call him in case it somehow gave something away, in case they were watching or listening. I took the tiny card from the back of the phone and snapped it in two between my teeth and my forefingers before tossing it under the seats in front.

The world sliding by in a haze reminded me of the journey from Paris which, although not so different, had seemed much more hopeful than this one. This was the final leg one way or another and anyone who thought it was anything less than a death match was wrong. Only one party was coming back from this; all I could do was pray and hope it was me.

I survived the bus journey and pulled my hood up over my head to tackle the train station which was more than alive with people doing much more exciting things, simple things. There were commuters in sharp suits, hipsters with retro cameras and strange hats, and mothers herding rebellious children. The air smelled of coffee and newspaper and, well, just normality. The dark underbelly of the world was not even a consideration for these people and I was so envious my stomach ached but my envy turned to drive. I was doing this for all of them too, I had to remember that every time I felt like I wanted to run a million miles away.

The departure boards were like a night sky, too many

lights to follow and changing constantly. I finally saw it, my train and, despite having plenty of time, I ran, so fast. I needed to get there, away from the risk that crowds posed. I pushed my way through hordes of people and gasped more than once at an ill-timed shoulder barge or extended glare. People stared all the time but when you were me it took on a whole new meaning. Every overzealous people-watcher was a potential threat.

Again, I picked an advantageous seat with a decent view of my carriage. There were lots of people around - none of them looked threatening, but wasn't that the whole point? My eyes darted in every direction and I knew I wouldn't be able to drop my guard for a second. Six hours of panic, not the kind of Zen state I had hoped for... I needed to prepare, to think, to be ready to do anything it took.

I fidgeted uncomfortably in my seat, the sitting version of pacing a room, and toyed with an empty water bottle that lay on the table in front of me. With no-one near with a decent view, I turned the phone to hands-free, stood it on end and in a particularly intense moment shattered it into sharp, icy shards. Several fell to the floor by my feet... one even imbedded in the rubber seal for the window. I plucked it out quickly and stowed it on the floor with the rest. The remaining pieces clung to the air as if suspended on my breath and I held them, toying with them as I lowered them to the table and then swept them covertly away.

I turned my attention back to what mattered; the people

that I was sharing this tin can with and what they may or may not know about me. I focused my attention on the couple across from me. They seemed oblivious to me but I stared intently at their loving glances and gentle touches of each other. As I lost myself in their world, I started to hear them, hear the things they weren't saying to each other and it proved again that appearances are not always what they seem.

She was stroking the back of his hand with her fingers and outwardly they seemed so perfectly aligned with each other. But her mind was screaming something else. She was trying to wipe away her sadness; she didn't trust him, she knew she was right not to trust him and she was desperately trying to pretend it was working. The deep, gut-wrenching sadness was tangible and it was lodged like a lump in my throat that I just couldn't swallow. I wanted to reach out for her and when tears swelled in my eyes I knew I had to move on.

The man just behind them was almost out of view, but he was shadowing my own desire to stay private. Holed up in the comfort of an oversized hoodie. Another surprise though; because I had listened once, it got easier and when I managed to drown out the anxiety of Romeo and Juliet in front, I could just hear his concern. His mother was sick, he was on his way to visit her, praying for enough time to say goodbye. So much sadness surrounded me and it further compacted the oddness of everything. None of us ever knew what other people were faced with; you would think with that in mind we would be nicer to each other, but no.

Three hours in, the doors between carriages slid open with a whoosh and a woman probably the same age as my mom stood there; for a little too long. She hovered staring the length of the carriage and I felt a surge of panic. It was instinctive. She looked completely average... mousy brown hair pulled into a loose ponytail, skinny jeans tucked into smart riding boots and she wore a wrap cardigan. I don't know what it was that caught my attention, but something didn't feel right at all. She didn't move, she just seemed to be searching. I pulled my hood further over my head and tucked my dangerously recognizable hair into it. I took out my phone as a decoy... I needed to look like every other teenager in the world, engrossed in social media and socially unavailable all at the same time. She started to move, slowly, gazing into each seat row as she went and for whatever reason I just felt like it was for me. My heart raced and I thought about fleeing but if she was looking for me I would just be lighting the beacon and it wasn't like I could really go far on a moving train.

As she approached my table I started to feel hot and sick. My brain went into overload and I searched for an idea to help me out of the situation. She grew closer and closer and my hands twitched under the tabletop. Use them my brain chanted, use the powers, but I was terrified of hurting anyone else, I wasn't prepared enough to practice close range like this.

She reached where I was sitting and I stared out of the window, my still exterior at complete contrast to how I was feeling inside. The growling dark within me jeered and heckled... do it. Do it now. I forced myself to regulate my breathing and not even look up.

She paused. I thought about turning and acting but I was frozen, I didn't have what it took. This was it; I wasn't going to get to where I needed. But then something amazing happened, she stopped alongside me and cleared her throat and I was sure I'd be sick, then she spoke.

"Gretchen?!" Her voice broke, she was welling up. I pulled down my hood against all my better judgment and watched as her face fell. She dissolved into tears and I was confused. If she was after me and playing some sort of game she was the most convincing actor yet.

"Sorry... no." She slid into the seat opposite me and sobbed into her hands. What was going on? The fear had temporarily gone and I was bemused.

"I'm so sorry. I thought..." she sobbed again.

I leaned in, eager to offer some comfort; she was obviously very distressed. What was I doing? Crying convincingly did not mean she wasn't dangerous. But, something took over and I suddenly felt like I needed to help her.

"I thought you were my daughter. She is about your age. She has been missing for three weeks and I, I don't know what to do. I just keep searching." It seemed that I had been wrong, I was rusty and on edge and I had been so very wrong.

I reached over the table and held her hand; it just seemed like the right thing to do. But in that instant, it was like all the power within my head mainlined through me into our touching fingers. In that moment I somehow saw it all… the fight they had been having, about her daughter's choice of boyfriend of all things. The storming out, the police, more tears and an empty bed, which a mother desperately wanted to fill again. Then something unusual and not so like my previous experiences… I saw her, this Gretchen. I don't even know how I knew it was her, but I did, I was sure. She was with the boy; they were in a car pulling into a hotel lot. I saw the sign and mentally snapshotted the name.

I could have sworn she felt something while I held her hand as she was swept over with a wave of calm. The crying stopped and she held my gaze with such hope in her eyes.

"I know this sounds ridiculous and I can't explain it, but I think I know where she might be. I just have this really strong feeling and I think it's worth checking out. I know this sounds insane."

She didn't run a mile. She just asked calmly…"Tell me, please tell me?"

"I think she is at the AirportHotel in Schipol… I can't

explain, I just feel it." She nodded, mouthed a silent thank you and pulled out her phone as she moved back to the vestibule. That was the first time I felt like I had used the gift to really help someone. She disappeared and I was left with the calmest sensation I had felt in some time.

I watched her through the glass door as she spoke on the phone, to her husband maybe, the police? Then she disappeared out of sight. It felt like fate had just dealt me a chance to feel good, like there was a point to all this, a reason why I had these powers and that it could be used for real good. Like there might be life afterwards where I could channel my new found energy into positivity instead of pain and torment.

TRACKING

I breathed a lengthy sigh of relief as the train coasted to a stop in Strasbourg. I had made it here at least and bar my not-so-near miss on the train, there seemed little reason to be concerned. Hopefully this meant, if there was any hope, that Jean had de-railed their ability to track me. I had been working really hard on keeping my brain locked tight from Alice, from Elias. But Jake, I had no idea where he was and the weight of the worry was starting to manifest itself. I had itchy welts on my skin; all up my arms resembled a bee keeping mission gone wrong. It was stress and I knew it. Jake, where the hell are you? The words were like a screensaver passing through my overcrowded brain. They kept coming full circle and flashing by my eyes. I had to get there before him. There was no choice.

There were still four days before the meeting I had seen in my vision. Jean had managed to hack into the administration system for the European Parliament building and had painstakingly gone through all the records to ascertain what rooms were in use and when. It was testament to what he was capable of... I was pretty sure not just anyone could hack through that level of security. Four days, four days to find Jake and derail his insane plans, whatever they were and then the small, non-stressful matter of saving everyone I knew, perhaps everyone period.

I decided the lower I could lay the better for the next few days. I managed to find somewhere suitably down market to set up camp. I almost enjoyed checking-in under an alias, kind of felt fun and rebellious, but as ever when there was light in my situation, it was short lived. Seconds after throwing my bag onto a questionable bedspread, I found myself slumped between the bed and the wall as my body convulsed with a vision. It was short and painful. I was feeling Jake's pain, he was hunched somewhere equally dingy and he was crying silently. My eyes joined in in sympathy and longing and from within the vision I felt a lump rise in my throat. I couldn't see where he was but I knew, at least for now he wasn't there, with them or even trying to get in anywhere he shouldn't. Seeing him in such pain was worse than feeling it myself but this vision showed me I had time to find him. I searched desperately in the dark for any hints of where he was but the only thing I could hear was music. The distant pulse of a baseline and I thought I could smell strong liquor, but I didn't get the chance to really dig, it all went dark before I could deduce anything else.

Ok, a young guy in or near a bar with music… that's a needle in a thousand mile haystack if ever there was one. I sighed deeply and reclined onto the bed. Against my better judgment and previous thoughts on the matter I decided to call him, but no cells, too easy to track, too dangerous. I padded back down the dimly lit hall of the hostel and into the lobby to use the pay phone. I picked up the receiver and recoiled at its state. I rubbed the mouthpiece down on my sweater before I dared use it. Gross.

I dialed the last number I could remember for him; Jean had confiscated his normal cell too in a bid to maintain our top secret lair, i.e. his home.

My fingers trembled as I pressed the suspiciously sticky key pad and I winced in disgust. I swallowed hard and waited for the dial tone, even that was a strange and small reminder that we were far from home. The tone held out, good news; at least the number was in use. Why did everything feel like an eternity when you so desperately wanted to speak to someone important? My head was flooded with pre-emptive conversation… should I be mad?

Upset? Relieved if he answered? The whole time the phone was ringing my head buzzed a familiar way. I knew it was Elias trying to reach me and my concern for him was almost enough to make me break my own rules and let him in, but he was trying to contact me, so he was alive. Right now I had to focus on the plan and find Jake. I brought down the wall, closed my mind to him with a silent apology. I didn't hear it but I knew he was cursing me. If there was one thing he couldn't stand it was not getting his own way. I could practically sense his blood boiling across the distance.

I snapped back into the moment when the dial tone stopped. The line wasn't dead, it had been answered but there was no voice, just shallow breaths as if the phone was being held at length. I hated that I couldn't tell who it was. I almost hung up, sure that if it was him he would have spoken, but maybe he knew what was coming, most of all I was annoyed that if it was him I should know.

I quickly grew tired of the waiting and forced the sound from my dry throat.

"Is it you?" I held off on saying his name, just in case. Caution was my drug these days, it kept me alive. The silence continued for a bit longer and the tension mounted in correlation with my escalating heart rate.

"Scarlett... I..." A wave of warm relief rushed through me, followed almost immediately by an intense rage.

"What the hell, Jake? Where the hell are you? What

were you thinking?" The line was silent again; he knew he was in deep and rightly worried.

"Look I just wanted to track down Elias and see if the two of us couldn't sort something out, try limit your involvement. This situation is no place for you. And I think…"

I didn't know whether to be touched by the sentiment or outraged at the hypocrisy and sexism of it all. I went with the latter.

"NO. Just No, Jake. You didn't think at all and that is the problem. Are you serious? This situation is no place for you… you can't save me or anyone else. It isn't your fight, it's mine. I want you safe so I get to come back to you. I don't want some stupid, misplaced heroism to take you away from me. It makes no sense."

"Wow… so you really don't think I can help at all do you? My dad was one of these things, I know enough and I sure as hell know how to protect my girlfriend…"

"Remove your ego from this situation, Jake. Stop making it a pissing contest between you and Elias. I don't want him to save me either. I need to do this alone, it's the only way." I heard his exasperated exhalation down the line. "You and him, you are just minor collateral damage to them, but not to me. I only have hope, a reason to try at all, if I have you to come back to, don't you see?"

"Ok, ok, I get it. I should have spoken to you first. But please, don't keep pushing me away. I understand what you're saying but you have to see how hard this is for me too. Turn this around; would you be so happy to let me walk into this, away from you, into such danger? I don't think so." He made a valid point and my silence confirmed it. I had to see him. The madness had receded and I wanted to hold him, be held, just be and forget for a moment.

"Where are you? I'm coming to find you." The idea that we could be close warmed me and my stomach leapt in the right kind of way.

"NO, stay put. You shouldn't be wandering around on your own. I'll come find you. What's the name of the place you're staying?" I took the address from a worn out sticker on the phone and he worked out where he was in relation to me.

"I'll be with you in about twenty minutes." His voice had lifted too and the tension and spark was palpable down the line. I hung up and went to change.

My disgust toward my room had faded in the anticipation of being reunited with Jake but as twenty minutes came and went - then thirty, then forty-five my excitement turned to panic. He should have been here by now.

I didn't dare leave in case he arrived and I didn't know where to look as he never said where he was but I couldn't stay. I waited another excruciating five minutes before I scrawled a note and stuck it on my door with my gum and ran out into the streets. I had no bearings, no real idea of where to go but the feeling in the pit of my stomach seemed to respond to my fleeing feet. I took lefts and rights and had no regard for whom or what may have seen me. I needed to find Jake, right at that moment there was nothing else.

I felt the thud of my shoulders as they collided with passers-by. I shoved and heaved my way through confused faces and muggy alien streets. A stray cat, black fur all matted and filthy passed in front of me and I stopped dead. Was that good luck? Cats and luck, who was I kidding? Nothing like that made any blind bit of difference anymore. I was out of breath, exhausted and I needed a break but I couldn't stop; I couldn't afford the time.

I picked up the pace again as I ran by a line of stores and the entrance to a small alley. I was about three store fronts down before the feeling overwhelmed me. I had to turn back, I knew I had gone too far, there was just a weight in me that told me I had to. I spun on my heels and doubled back to the same alley. The height of the buildings darkened the path even in day light. I felt a familiar feeling rise inside me as I stepped tentatively into the space; navigating between waste bags and discarded packaging I scoured the path ahead until it ended with another building's fire escape. It was all just trash; I couldn't see anything but the feeling would not leave me. I was meant to be there but I couldn't tune into anything else, there was no detail, just an urge, screaming at me to stay.

I took another few steps and let out a shrill scream as I tripped backwards over what I thought was just some discarded cartons. My heart pounded and I saw the glances I attracted from the street beyond. I froze until they went about their business, I did not need any extra attention right now.

Exhausted from running and terrified of what I was heading towards, I slumped against the wall to catch my breath. I took a shaky step and that was when I heard it. It was weak and barely there but it was a voice.

My eyes darted left and right but I couldn't see the owner of that sound. It was distorted and coarse and more pained than I'd ever heard which was saying something. I frantically pulled debris from the floor around my feet. I yanked a piece of board, maybe three feet long and heaved it to the other side of my body.

My eyes struggled to acclimatize to the poor light and for a brief second I thought I had misheard and there was nothing. It looked like just another mountain of life's leftovers. Then I saw it; a hand sketched in bright crimson.

My body let out a sob and I dragged away the trash and boxes. I wasn't prepared for what I would find and my heart felt like it may implode with sadness. If it wasn't for what I felt it wouldn't have been the sight of him that confirmed it; he was barely recognizable. His face bloodied and swollen. His right eye was forced shut and blood poured from a deep cut across his forehead. His perfect lips had been broken and split and his blood spattered from his mouth with every labored breath. I collapsed to my knees and reached out for his hand. His knuckles were bloodied and fat from the fight, he had tried to protect himself but it was clear he was outmatched and by more than one person.

Breath hissed from his lips and his shirt heaved as it concealed what sounded like breathing from within broken ribs. His jeans were shredded, if I wasn't sure what had done this I would have guessed a wild animal. They were frayed and torn, his legs covered in slash marks and more rivulets of blood; the denim was drenched and heavy.

I pulled his weak, unsupported torso onto my knees and wept. He tried to speak but I shushed him with my finger; frightened to touch him.

"Baby... shh. Don't speak. Shhh now." I rocked him gently with huge tears coursing down my cheeks. This was my fault. This was a message for me and Sanguinaries didn't do subtle.

I kept trying to speak, to apologize but the words were lost in grief and the weight of the sight. My beautiful Jake was buried beneath the scars of knowing me; loving me came at such a high price, I wasn't sure I could let him do it anymore. In fact I knew it was pure selfishness to even consider it.

"I, I'm ok." His breath spattered blood on my hands as they rested on his chest. I was doused in his pain and we both reeled in silent shock.

"This isn't ok, Jake. You are not ok. I am getting you safe and then I'm fixing this. It can't go on and I will not watch the life drain from you for knowing me."

"Loving." He whispered.

"What?"

"I don't know you, Scarlett. I love you. This isn't your fault. I chose this, I chose you and I stand by every second. I still would, even if I thought I'd bleed out right here and now because pain is transient. I don't regret a second of this because you are home. Being with you is home to me and I see that now more than ever. You're my family."

I didn't have the words to respond. I was relieved, humbled, privileged and swept away by what he had said and I knew I had to stop pushing against him. That's what had gotten us here. Every time I pushed him away, something terrible happened. If I kept him with me there were risks but I could use my powers to protect him. He was too vulnerable alone and too much like bait; they know they can use him to get me. It was time to offer myself and see what happened.

I held him until the air blew cold around us and I noticed he was shivering. I draped my jacket over his shoulders and helped him to his feet. His legs gave way several times before we managed to get him upright and he bit hard on his lip to contain his pain but I could feel it resonating through his tight grip on my forearm.

We left the sheltered light of the alley and the extent of

his injuries was made clear. It was somehow even worse than I thought and in the time that had lapsed his face was more swollen and blood caked in his nostrils and the corners of his eyes.

Passers-by either stared or hid their gaze but no-one offered to help. We hailed a cab and I dredged the address of my hostel from my memory. I was taking him with me. The cab driver muttered something under his breath disapprovingly. I knew we should have been taking him to a hospital but we couldn't risk it; I had to do the best I could for him.

Luckily the hostel entrance was abandoned, no-one sat on reception and the stairwell was ours. I held him close as we fought to make the ascent. Every step was agony and he was faltering.

Once back in the relative sanctuary of my room I draped the bed with towels and laid him down. I took out the small first aid kit I had been carrying since our journey began and hurriedly tipped its limited contents on to the bed.

I had butterfly stitches, some antiseptic wipes, gauze and a few bandages. It wasn't great but it was all we had. I brought out a wet flannel and a large bowl that was being used to catch drips falling from the leaking bathroom ceiling. I rinsed it out and filled it with warm water. I started trying to reveal his face from beneath the crimson veil of blood. He writhed and tensed beneath my touch and I bit my lip to stop from crying as I wrung out the cloth and the water ran red. Slowly his face was revealed and I could start cleaning the wounds. I worked slowly, as tenderly as I could. The cut above his eyebrow was deep and jagged. I rinsed it, and pushed through his stifled screams and moans. I used some of the sticky strips to bring it back together and held them in place for moment. I wiped a tear that coursed down his cheek away without a word and kept on.

It took more than an hour of excruciating dressing and cleaning before I was done. He nearly passed out from pain on more than one occasion and my heart felt weak with guilt and the longing for simplicity in my life.

I cut the jeans from his body and gasped as I pulled them away and saw his skin blotted with deep purple bruising. I gently removed his shirt and cast it aside on the floor with the rest. From his collarbone to his pelvis there was little more than a few inches of skin that held his normal complexion. I stopped for a moment and stroked his head. He was settling now, the worst was over. As long as he stayed still it wasn't so bad. My hands moved as light as a feather over his pain and I gently decorated his torso with kisses. He lifted a weak hand to mine and pulled me into him. I nestled alongside him cautiously and felt his body start to relax.

As he drifted in and out of a broken sleep, I gathered up his things. The jeans were probably ruined, there was so much blood soaked into the fabric. I held out his shirt, it wasn't much better but I know he didn't have much with him so I headed to the tiny sink to see what magic I could work. As I moved the worst hit areas towards the running faucet, a tiny square of paper fell to the floor. As I unfolded the page, I saw the chicken scrawl handwriting and I didn't really need to look closer; I could have almost guessed the wording itself, let alone who left it for me. And it was for me.

Browning blood obscured some of the letters, but the message was still pretty clear.

We guessed you might be looking for him and we wanted to make it clear this was our show. Always our show. You're next. V.

The image of them all sitting around, discussing what they would do with Jake, to him, made my blood run cold. Of course they would use him as a way to get to me but it had to stop. Even though I promised not to push him away, I had to think of a new approach. I couldn't drag him with me; they weren't playing when they left him in that alley.

I was barely asleep the whole night. I just laid there watching him, making sure the rise and fall of his chest never slowed, that his pained breaths kept coming and that every time he howled in pain I was ready to hold him, comfort him. It was the longest night I could remember since the asylum and it felt worse because the person suffering was Jake.

When morning broke I left him sleeping to go grab

some food and I used the cool air on my face to focus. I had three days now until the meeting, but they knew I was here or at least that I would be eventually. They hadn't taken long to work out wherever Jake went I was sure to follow. It would be so much easier if I could just turn off my humanity the way they did, disassociate. It was my humanity that made me weak; emotions, confusion, guilt, responsibility, a desperate need to help. I had three days only to try and achieve it, that level of commitment to my cause, something so strong that I could forgo all things that I cared about. I was stalling because I knew that this time, these days, were possibly my last and the thought of no further time with Jake, my mom, Lydia, Taylor, hell, even Elias; it was too much to bear. The alternative was worse. Lost in my thoughts and knowledge was the potential for what havoc they could wreak if I caved, if they could control me, the things they could do. Countries would fall, people would die and I'd be the beginning of the end somehow.

When I got back Jake was sitting up, he looked slightly less pale and his good eye had regained some of that familiar brightness. I tossed him a bottle of pain killers I picked up at the grocery store. He half smiled, then immediately winced before unscrewing the cap and practically inhaling a handful of the tablets. He beckoned for the coffee in my hand and downed the pills in one gulp.

"You look... better. Kind of. How you feeling?"

"Well, for someone who probably should have died yesterday, not too shabby." His ability to make light of even the harshest situations astounded me. He smirked and patted the bed next to him. I shuffled in and passed him his bagel. I took mine from its paper bag but couldn't face more than pitifully picking the raw edges where the knife had cut it in two.

"Don't say that. If you'd…"

"Shh. Don't even. We are not getting back into the whole 'I shouldn't be involved' thing. You know you would be doing the exact same if this scenario were reversed so let's move on. What's your plan? He was wearing his boss persona and I liked it, I'd missed it and what it did to me. It also marked some kind of understanding and felt like he knew the games were over, that there was no room anymore for heroics, this was my show now. I sounded like them.

"Plan? Well… I had Jean lead them away, make them think I am further from here, but what happened to you yesterday suggests they either didn't buy it or they are hoping to draw me here regardless, so whichever it is we have to lay low. You especially. I do not want a repeat of this. OK?"

"So, what does that mean for you? What about Elias and Alice, they must know you are here, doesn't that compromise everything? Especially with you and him and all that special code talking you do."

I felt my face fall. I knew Jake knew we could do it, but he had never referenced it so blatantly.

"I am blocking them out as much as I can but it's hard. I can feel Elias trying to get in but I don't know if they are making him or he is trying to check in. Either way I am holding him at bay until such time as it doesn't matter anymore."

"What does that mean... doesn't matter anymore?" His face was etched with concern now. He hated it when I started talking serious, even if it was in response to a question.

"Well in three days they are coming together to discuss me, sell me, which means they need and expect to have me by then. So they are going to get me." I stared at the floor as I felt his body tense beside me.

"You're just going to hand yourself in? Scarlett..." I held up my hand in defense of my own point.

"Wait... listen. They need me in that room or they will have some pretty pissed comic villains on their hands. So, I know they are coming for me, one way or another. This is fact. The stuff I can change is how they get me, when they get me and, most importantly, what happens when they do."

His one good eye rolled in his head and I could have put money on the words that would follow. So, I didn't let them.

"Things have changed since they last had me. I've

changed, Jake. For all they know about me, my weaknesses… they don't know what I can do now. All they know is the potential. They think part of the deal is they get to unlock it, but they're wrong. All that time in Amsterdam I was doing that myself. I am already dangerous in ways they haven't even imagined." His grip tightened around my hand and I flashed him a small, but strong smile. "I can do this. I have to."

COUNTDOWN

"So, what? You're going to just walk in there? Powers blazing and take them down? Sounds dangerous and a little reckless to me." If I didn't know him better I'd say he didn't believe in me, but I was fairly confident this was the fear talking.

"No. I know that they're coming and one way or another they'll find me. When they do, I'll let them drag me in. I am not going to storm in there. It is crucial to the outcome that they think I am still terrified of them, well I am but, that they think I am not in control enough. If I can just convince them that I'm little old frightened Scarlett and keep them feeling in charge, then I have a chance."

He nodded. He had seen what I could do now. I wished I could have shown him what was in me, the parts even I hadn't discovered. I had this overriding feeling that even after Amsterdam there was more to come and that I just hadn't figured it all out yet. If that was the case then I was potentially very dangerous to them.

"Jake, I need to ask you to do something for me, something which I know will be really tough but it is so important and I need you to trust that I know it's the right thing." His expression defined solemnity, his posture fell. I knew he knew what I was about to ask. He met my gaze.

"Go on."

"When I go I don't want you to follow me. I need to know you are out of the way."

"But..."

"No, Jake. No buts. This isn't about me thinking you can't do anything; don't let your ego rule on this one. This is about me needing to focus, and I can't do that if I think you're in danger. I need a clear head. Can you do this for me?"

He was shaking his head and his body language was fraught. "I just..."

"Thank you. I love you so much. I just need to do this." We didn't speak for a while, the conversation kind of reverberated between us.

We lost the day keeping Jake upped with pain killers and

laughing about dorky memories from Salem. He reminded me of the day we met outside the hall in town when I had just moved. He laughed at my awkwardness.

"You were so uncomfortable talking to me... it was adorable." He smiled and I couldn't help but join in. "I mean you still are, but all this power to take over the world stuff makes you a bit less little girl lost and a bit more kick ass."

"I take it kick ass and adorable don't mix?" I cozied up to him playfully, cautious not to get too close and touch his bruises.

"Oh, they mix alright. You're still adorable, just now you're a little more, well, worldly and that kind of makes you sexier!" He pulled me on to him with a wince and a sharp intake of breath. I knew he was struggling but my concern was dwarfed by my desire for him and the pull of his mouth against mine.

We lost two days between practicing and bed. There was no doubt that the tension for what loomed laid heavy in the air and it changed us both; kisses lingered, hands held tighter, hugs were more like fear-drenched goodbyes but we kept smiling. We had to.

I dreamt of Alice and Elias both nights. I could never tune in though, even asleep I refused to risk everything, so lingered like some kind of subconscious trespasser but one thing remained the same; the sense that someone, perhaps the reaper, was always close behind. Whoever, or whatever, it had sucked the light from what I could see, it was like wading through shadows or wearing blinkers; all I knew was that it wasn't good. Most likely it was a representation of the growing sense of foreboding I felt.

Jean and I had discussed a change in the trail when it was time and a brief message to him at the right moment meant he was already leading them closer to me, all I had to do now was be in the right place at the right time.

Jake and I hadn't really discussed what we would do when that moment came, the one that would see me walk out and leave him there to wonder about me and hope. I had thought about it though and little else. I knew if the situation were reversed there was no way I would listen to him. I would break my promise in that instance and do everything I could to be part of it, to help and make sure that whatever happened we would be together and yet I expected him to do the opposite. It was unfair to ask but I needed to try and I hoped that his current state meant it was more likely for him to stay put, he was in no shape to fight.

I dragged together what little stuff I had and pulled my bag onto my shoulder. Jake returned from the bathroom to find me ready to go, jacket on and I swallowed the lump already building in my throat as I watched his face fall.

I walked over to him in the doorway, his posture limp, lost, broken.

"I love you." He nodded into the crook of my neck and inhaled slowly. He kissed me silently and we both chose not to make any remark about the tears I felt course down my skin or the stain of dark blue on his pale blue shoulder. The silence clung to the small space left between us and screamed all of the words we were both thinking. I refused to acknowledge the possibilities in front of me, bar one: the one that said it could work, I could win and I would get back to him.

He gripped my hand as I stepped away and stopped my already reluctant progress. I pressed the bracelet into his palm. "Take care of it for me."

I held my breath for fear he was about to bring the wall tumbling down with some of the words we promised not to speak, but instead he simply pulled my hand to his lips and placed a single kiss on the third finger of my left hand and whispered: "Come back to me."

More tears, previously quashed, streamed down my face as I lifted the dead weight of my feet from the room. I hadn't looked back at him, I couldn't because it was taking all of me to move at all and his expression, like the one where I told him I was going ahead of him to Paris or when Elias kissed me, that sad, lost, but ultimately drenched in love expression was going to cloud my judgment and throw me off. I couldn't afford it, not this time.

I felt the cold air hit the tears on my face and had to pause to pull myself together. I needed be about four blocks away in the next ten minutes, exactly where Jean had made out I would be. This was it.

I stepped forward into the fading light and into my future with blind hope that not only did they not know the full extent of my abilities, but that, perhaps, I didn't either.

MARK

My phone vibrated in my breast pocket. It was Jean, just the letter x, meaning they were headed to me and as the mark, I needed to be there soon. It was supposed to be subtle, nothing out of the ordinary, so the credit card trail had been rigged to put me on a relatively quiet street.

I turned the corner and faced the location of my 'capture'. A small late night coffee bar was illuminated against the dim street and this was it. This tiny innocuous place was where they were coming to find me.

I slid into a window seat and, when the small, dark haired waitress came over, I ordered a coffee I knew I wouldn't drink. When she returned I picked up the spoon and dragged it round and round in the froth, staring into it intently, desperately trying to focus my mind and avoid succumbing to the potential for terror.

My head was still down and my eyes fixed, but I felt it happen; the atmosphere changed in a split second. My heart picked up pace and I looked behind me to the sparse scattering of customers, trying to assess if it was just me that felt it. There were no concerned glances, no whispered worries, just people getting on with life in a series of inane and perfectly normal ways.

The air definitely felt colder, the skin on my arms and neck grew tight and the skin puckered from my forearm to my wrist in a slow, chilling motion.

I looked up and faced the dark street. Once my eyes discounted the coffee shop lights reflecting in the glass I could see the road in front of me. Two dark shapes moved in unison from across the street. I pulled in my breath despite my chest feeling like it was being compressed. This was them, the messengers, the Sanguinaries tasked with delivering me back to them. I had to make it believable, I had to run.

I paused and watched them edge closer; their steps were slow and purposeful. They were entirely confident in their ability to deliver, which meant there was a careful plan, they wouldn't risk losing me again.

My breath was caught in my chest, I needed the perfect

moment. They were yards away when I exhaled and slowly raised my head. My eyes caught those of the one on the right. He was larger and even more unnaturally broad than the henchmen I had met previously; they were pulling out the real hunters now.

I widened my eyes, not as a charade, the fear was real. The corners of his mouth turned up and exaggerated the scar that ran from below his nose to his chin, we all knew this was it and I just made this their biggest hunt ever. I stood up, the coffee left untouched was upturned by my flailing jacket and the clatter of the cup against the saucer and then the bench was enough to draw the attention of the entire place.

I pushed through the door with no more than three meters between me and them. I started to run, probably faster than I ever had in my life. Even though I knew capture was inevitable, essential even, I couldn't fight the urge to try. My legs circled and blood pumped noisily in my ears as my feet created dull, rhythmic thumps against the pavement. I didn't dare look back but I didn't need to, they weren't running yet, they were eerily calm and slow. I took a left down a smaller street; they'd get me here for sure.

I leaned against a bare brick wall, my chest aching for some respite. I saw their shadows before they reached me and watched as the black twisted shapes were connected to the feet of my soon-to-be captors.

I heard their breathing and went to take off again, but before I could even engage my feet, it was like they had teleported to me. They covered the ground so fast, they were there, inches away. Lucky for my instincts it was necessary for the ruse that I put up a bit of a fight, so I closed my eyes and drew everything I could to push them back... I drew on every moment in the house in Amsterdam but it wasn't enough, my half-in half-out state of mind wasn't focused enough. Then I found it. I looked to the image of Jake lying bloody in that alley and it was instant. With the extension of my hands they were forced back a few meters. I kept it light, but I knew that thought was enough to total the immediate area if I was to let loose. Good to know.

They rose again from the wall to which they had been momentarily pinned. Now both wearing matching smirks, they inched forward as I took to run. It disturbed me how totally unfazed they were. If they knew what I had done in the catacombs and weren't concerned about their ability to capture me it could only mean one thing: they had their own plan.

One extension of a huge arm and he had me, but I struggled loose, two, maybe three times. I stumbled and fell and everything went fuzzy. I had hit my head and was woozy but in many ways it helped, it stopped me from losing it and taking them down right there. There were restraints; my body was dragged a little before being hulked over a huge shoulder. The motion made me nauseous. I closed my eyes wearing a strange smile… relief maybe? Or the promise of revenge. Either way it was working, they felt in charge and for the first time in a long while, I knew they were wrong about something.

By the time I felt stable enough to fully open my eyes, the van had stopped and they were opening the doors. Light flooded in, artificial, fluorescent light, which sent a throbbing pain across my head from temple to temple. I shielded my eyes with my hand and winced as I moved; my wrist was sore, raw and red. I looked down to see a wide and thick metal cuff closed tight against my skin. It wasn't a restraint though; it wasn't attached to anything else. It was smooth and simple and the only defining feature was a tiny black box with a red light. I tugged at the cuff but it was so tight and fused together, there was no natural way to remove it, though they knew full well this wouldn't be a problem after last time. I focused on the band and exhaled in concentration.

"I wouldn't do that if I were you." The muscle finally used his mouth. I looked up and he was wearing that smug expression again.

"Wouldn't do what exactly?" I responded with just enough sass that they would recognize I was putting up a fight but didn't hold eye contact for too long… it had to be real and I was intrigued.

"Come on. Drop it. We know" He looked to his

companion and they shared a knowing glance.

"What do you think you know about me?" I maintained the fear factor by actively retreating into the van. The silent one reached in and yanked me forward by the arm. He caught the cuff and I let out an unintentional howl of pain which seemed to amuse them. They really were like wild dogs. So thirsty for blood and fear.

"Enough. We know you think that you might feel like blowing that thing off your wrist and making a run for it. But we strongly advise against it... that said, might be amusing to watch you see what happens when you do." He hissed the words through crooked teeth, no doubt shifted through blow after blow with various adversaries on their behalf. He was another mongrel, bred for violence, no fixed abode. He had no discernible accent, his voice was just rage and bitterness.

"What is it?" I pulled at it again but it only dug further and further into my skin. My eyes welled at the pain and I sense their anticipation. They were turned on by my pain.

"Let's just say if you decide to try anything like last time; any escape, any thoughts you might have on blowing us up or leaving us for dead and running home, that bracelet will, either by your actions or our command, result in some, how should I put it? Explosive consequences."

I glared back, my mind scrambling to think of what their hand was this time. It wasn't Jake and they knew already that Elias and I had an understanding, I wouldn't

144

risk everyone else they could hurt for him, he wouldn't want to let me. So what? Then the most horrific realization washed over me. There wasn't much left for them to play against me, but it wasn't what, it was who. My blood ran ice cold and I watched their expressions and how their puckered, gnarled faces stretched and contorted with glee when they saw me connect the dots.

"You can't have. I made sure." My voice broke and I wasn't acting anymore. They grinned back, nothing behind their eyes but the desire to hurt.

"Not sure enough." With that they dragged me out into the light and the building rage in my chest threatened to overpower me. I had to pull it back, save all this for when I really needed it. My powers were building; there was a silent storm swirling and gathering pace within my chest and it felt like I was trying to contain something bigger, something celestial almost. I had never known it this strong, not even when I had burned off my shackles in Paris. Something was changing in me.

I looked down at the cuff and its threat and bottled every atom of the resentment and hatred it planted within me and buried it, deep inside. I looked up at them and wiped the tears from my cheeks and complied.

The van was backed right up against an exit, but I sensed it was right, we were there already, the Parliament building. It must have been some kind of security or service entrance. The walkway was a brightly lit tunnel punctuated with metal doors. I was trying to create some kind of mental map in case I should need to run at any point but it was a warren of pathways. Suppose a place where the leaders of the free world could come together had to have some secret escape routes. It wasn't lost on me, the irony of it all; leaders of the free world, almost all of whom I could bet would be here tomorrow to bid for me, their secret weapon, a ticking time bomb of power to unleash next time their neighbor disagreed with them. The world wasn't free, they were the puppet masters and people like me were resigned to a fate of dictatorship and persecution. Alice had given her life over to guiding me at whatever cost so that I could be The One to bring down their regime and I wouldn't let it be in vain, I couldn't.

They yanked the triple thickness chains attached to my cuffs and I sensed the difference; whatever they were made of they were more than the last; they were learning and adapting, just like me. The cuffs pressed hard into my skin and I winced as they led me to the end of a corridor. The light was dimmer here and the room was still in darkness. The click of the switch sent the room from pitch black to blinding white in an instant and the chains groaned as I instinctively shielded my eyes.

There was nothing in it. Nothing except a large chair, which looked suspiciously like the ones I had seen in movies, ones where people were on death row. This was an executioner's chair. I ought to have been flooded with panic, but the sense that they needed me had never been so strong; they may want the option to do it, but they wouldn't do it now.

I was hauled toward it rather unceremoniously and as soon as my back was against the hard upright panel, they stepped away. No more shackles, no belts, no extra chains. The only thing secured was my hands, other than that I could have just walked away. My captors backed up and exited the room without taking their eyes off me. The door slammed closed and I sat there in a kind of bemused silence. Why wouldn't I try to leave? There must be something; they were too on edge to risk it.

I looked around, the room was empty. Nothing. Nothing apart from the very distinct and unnerving sound of breathing. Loud, slow breathing. My own stopped in response, trapped in confused lungs, paralysed by the not knowing.

"Nice to have you back, Miss Roth." I could hear every tiniest lick of his tongue against his hideous teeth and my stomach lurched. It wasn't fear, it was repulsion. My skin itched thinking of any kind of proximity. Sutcliffe.

I looked around and I couldn't even see a camera lens. Then I spotted what must have been the speaker.

"I am sure you aren't surprised. You were always going to end up here. Kudos for your efforts though. You did give it a good shot." I clenched my jaw so hard the ache rippled through into my skull. I had to keep calm; save all of this for when it was really time. I exhaled my frustration, slowly and stowed the rage in my tightly balled fists.

"So, I am sure you have some little plot, a plan of escape and by all means, please, try. Though I am fairly sure our friends passed on your mother's regards and, well, it isn't really the time to go doing anything rash."

"Don't you dare, you bastard…" the words hissed though my teeth and I was mad at myself, for giving in. I let the rest of the words I had planned recede like a tide; back into the pit in my stomach.

"Now, now, Scarlett. We are all friends here, this is the modern age. There is no need for anyone to get over heated in this scenario. You simply play your part and she will be just fine."

I lowered my head as I tried to swallow down the tidal wave of anger. My mind couldn't help but wander to all the lives I knew were hanging in the balance and it was a selfish thought because I didn't mean The Collective, or the people yet to encounter The Venari. I was only thinking of my people, the ones I wanted to ensure I could keep after this was over. I wanted Jake, my mom, Elias, Alice, Celeste, Jean, Pierre.

As their faces passed before my mind's eye I pulled myself back from the precipice of losing it completely and composed my words and considered my tone carefully before I spoke.

"And what exactly is my part?"

"Well, I am glad you asked, Scarlett..." I could hear the curve of a smile in his voice and it sent a wave of anger through my hands as I tried to tame their shaking.

"Tomorrow, every major player in our organization and many, many more interested parties are coming here to, well, witness the extent of your powers. Some for curiosity, some for gain, some for the chance to be The One that ends it." He said it like it was nothing, like I was nothing. These freaks had been inhuman for so long, there was not a shred of a soul left to save.

"And if I don't play along with your stupid game of show and tell?" He let out an infuriating, drawn out laugh, which tailed off into an even more frustrating, smug sigh.

"Something tells me this time it is us that hold all the cards. It really isn't worth your efforts to fight." Then before I could respond, there was a thud like he dropped the microphone and I was plunged into the loudest silence of my life. I didn't know where Elias was, or Alice and I was too scared to check in with them in case it made them more vulnerable. They had my mom somewhere, God knows what they were doing or had done to her and I had left Jake alone. I needed my control back, but there was nothing to be gained in wasting what I had worked so hard to learn.

LOT

I didn't sleep. I think that was the plan. Leave me on edge in a well lit room as uncomfortable as possible. Whether or not they believed it would make me more 'pliable' I don't know, but the opposite was true. I had just spent, what I guessed was, about eight hours thinking, focusing on the outcome, their end, my victory and my chance to avenge the hundreds, maybe thousands that had gone before me.

When the door was unlocked I set my gaze on it, desperate to let go of the torrent of pent up readiness and desire to surge forward, just let it all out but I curbed everything and stowed my joy at the unsettling feeling of the rising tide within me. I was in control; I had to keep it that way.

Two new faces entered. How many of these muscled monsters did they have? Swathed in black coats they must have been boiling, these rooms were hotter than hell. The taller of the two grabbed me by my wrist, his fingers digging into my skin just above the cuff. I yanked my arm back but he grabbed me again before I could even blink and this time he held it even tighter, so tight I felt the bone creak under the pressure of his grip. He stared at me without a sound and spoke silently into my eyes. He looked like he might well be one of the ones that wanted to 'finish it', but it would be against the rules. The grunts don't get to have the glory here.

They dragged me through the maze of tunnels. After a while the sound of silence turned into a deep, low hum. It sounded like major machinery, rumbling and turning somewhere in the bowels of the building. I looked up at my 'walkers', that was what it felt like, like I was a dog on a warden's leash. The sound was getting louder as we mounted some metal stairs. We went up two, maybe three stories and exited the stark emptiness of the service corridors. Suddenly, we found ourselves in the real building, the one meant for bringing positive change and advancement to the world; the unbridled irony. They may as well have been walking me into the dark ages.

You could tell how these guys lived, how they were revered and pandered to wherever they went. The general areas were plush and comfortable and awash with well-made leather seating. All glass, chrome, light and expensive finishing touches. Absolutely no amount of tax-payers money was spared. This was a building designed for people who got what they wanted, period.

We trudged towards some doors flanked with airport-style security scanners. They shoved me through brashly and unsurprisingly my chains and cuffs sounded the alarm. Another of them appeared as if from nowhere and aggressively patted down my clothes. I shifted uncomfortably away as he lingered unreasonably long around my chest. The urge to drop him was almost unstoppable and the way the look on his face changed so suddenly when his eyes met mine suggested he felt a little tiny hint of what my mind was projecting.

In the commotion, I hadn't noticed that the machinery type noise I had been hearing before was here, where I was, and it wasn't the whir of air conditioning or generators; it was voices. So many voices. Even as I drew closer I couldn't determine the conversation but when the doors opened it was clear why.

The room was vast. Row upon row of seats, hundreds of them, arranged in a circular formation. One level up there were glass-fronted rooms like the hospitality boxes at concert stadiums and in every seat, behind that glass and on the floor of the immense hall, were hundreds of faces. The place was full and alive with an unnerving air of excitement. The sound of voices and various accents merged into a monotonous drone that probed deep into my mind with a dull ache. I shifted my hands to rub my temple and it was as if a school bell had rung. The sound of my chains resonated around the room and it was like a ripple on a pond. Row upon row of faces turned to witness the arrival of their 'prize'.

I watched as the whispers about my entrance swept through them. It was like viral interest; they were spinning around and craning their necks, practically falling over the backs of chairs to see me. When they did it was the same every time. Prolonged stares followed by greedy, hungry smiles. They were wolves and, in their eyes, I was the lamb.

Gasps and whispers of excitement gave way to silence and I could only presume they were deciding how much they were willing to bid. I was escorted through the parting crowds like some kind of celebrity towards a clearing in the seating. It was off center and more towards the back wall which housed a huge, authoritatively constructed section of seating clearly reserved for the biggest megalomaniacs.

There, in the middle, stood a huge glass chamber and another chair like the one in which I had been unfortunate enough to have to spend the previous night. An almost invisible door was pushed aside before one of my minders thrust me unceremoniously into the seat. It felt cold and hard beneath my clothes and I was suddenly acutely aware of the eyes of maybe six, seven hundred people boring into me. Some of their eyes were just wild, rabid and it felt better to just look down; it didn't hurt that it also made me look timid, afraid.

The door was replaced and all I could think was how humid it was. Dogs died in hot cars and I might die in an acrylic tube, in front of the best part of a thousand people who wanted to kill me... interesting.

It was strangely isolated despite the fact I was on show. The tube blocked out practically every tiny sound so what I saw looked like an old silent movie: lots of busy mouths but no sound. There were fingers pointing at me while others spoke animatedly to the people around them. I was watching them study me when a thud on the tube filled me with panic. My skin burned white hot and my breathing hitched; I felt the potential for defensive powers but I held them in, I had to. I looked to my left and a smartly dressed Chinese woman was right up against the glass, her face almost pressed upon it like a child staring into a toy shop. She studied me so intently and for the first time since I had put the plan in action I allowed myself to try flexing some muscles. I focused as hard as I could to see if I could hear anything and it was just one word. She had one, solitary thought amidst this chaos: 'Burn'.

Up until now I suppose I thought that really this was power not persecution, but there were a percentage of people here literally just to sentence me to death. I looked away and she crept below my eye line, desperate to hold my gaze. It felt sinister now and real. She just kept thinking it over and over until eventually her mouth joined in. Burn.

Not being able to hear started as a blessing but it began to feel infuriating and I was getting anxious in the close air. I had no idea what the time was, the clock behind me was in my blind spot and turning to face it pulled the cuffs too tight. The ocean of bodies bustled and stared until something changed. Their eyes moved in unison to something happening over my shoulder. Something had surpassed my power to fixate and they were drawn, practically salivating towards the raised seating that faced them from behind me: the VIP seats.

I think I already knew what it meant, or who, but I was in no rush to be proven right. I hadn't seen his face for a while but my mind was able to bring to life a more than adequate memory and that itself was enough to make me gag. His smirk, the flecks of food in his teeth when he would grip my face in his bony hand and speak so close I could feel the warmth of his putrid breath on my skin.

The lights dimmed slightly, the way they always did before the feature presentation. I allowed my eyelids to close slowly as I inhaled. The seating behind me was well lit and while I couldn't see them arriving, I felt the dull reverberation of several feet walking at once on the floor behind me. Then the click of an audio system, loud if I could hear it from my little cell as there were plenty of lips moving but I couldn't hear them.

There was a sudden whoosh of air and a click like the snapping of a branch. I looked up and four small slatted panels above my head that I hadn't even noticed before, parted to allow the room's air and accompanying noise into my pen. Thankfully the temperature dropped a couple of degrees as the air-conditioned atmosphere of the main hall took the place of the claustrophobic air of the container. The drone of a thousand voices was back but only for a second. A gavel sound rang out and, like children in an assembly, the waiting crowd fell silent again but shifted excitedly in their seats.

"Firstly, I want to thank you all for coming. I am quite sure the extended wait will be more than worth it. I know a great many of you have travelled considerable distance to join us and, I can assure you, you won't be disappointed."

His voice boomed with electronic assistance and hissed into every crevice of the room. The faces were no longer fixated on me, they were desperately clinging to his every word. If I hadn't known why I was there I would have thought them simple, rather than the likely megalomaniac masters of deception I knew they all were.

Some scrambled to position ear pieces, which I could only presume were the conduit of the translating of his venom into tens of other languages, making sure no one missed their instruction.

"I want to first run through some smaller matters of

business before we commence the viewing and, ultimately, the moment you have all been waiting for. the bidding." As the word left his mouth the room erupted into thunderous applause. Several of them stood, including two incredibly stern men to my right; I thought one was possibly Italian and the other looked like an Arab Sheikh. They were clapping with purpose, with a distinct sense of readiness.

"We will run through a short but telling demonstration in due course. There will be no requests and no additions to what is shown. Any requests will be ignored and the person in question may lose the right to bid. When bidding commences, we will take one bid at a time, this is a civilized transaction. We will deal in only full payment and bidders cannot co-share or co-own the lot. The winning bid will be paid immediately via wire transfer in a private room within this facility. Only upon completion and confirmation of the full transfer will we release the lot to the owners. There will be a car and or private jet made available, with full security measures, of course, for ease of exit and safe passage to your final destination. The unsuccessful bidders will have to leave immediately and personal items left on arrival can be collected at the entrance as you depart."

Lot? I wasn't a person here. I was wracking my brains, trying to figure out how the hell this thing would go down. Demonstration? I was clearly going to only have small windows of opportunity and I had to make the most of them. I took a cursory glance down to the cuffs weighing heavy on my wrists, almost covering the marks from the last episode, barely healed skin being worn through again. I felt the bitterness rise like a tide in my chest and I tried to keep my face zeroed on the crowd. If one pair of those eyes saw what I was doing it would be show time way before I was ready.

Staring at the cuffs I replayed Sutcliffe's words in my head. I just wanted a little reminder, a show of solidarity from my freakishness that it wasn't going to fail me when I needed it most. It was slower than normal, but it was there. A tiny tremor at first, then it dared to tremble and I felt the change. The metal was bending and softening around my wrists. Where it was pressing seconds before, it was now giving way to my wrist bone, relaxing around it like a mold. I shook it off and the metal hardened as I took a mental step back, but I knew I hadn't imagined it. The curve of the metal around my wrist was set differently, not how it started and I swallowed the sense of anticipation and the taste of fear. I was preparing for a war, the like of which I would have found impossible to imagine only a year or so ago, but I was different now. Stronger, smarter and brave enough to fight for the people that mattered. That was the whole point it seemed, to have something worth saving. Sure I was so scared at times I wasn't sure whether or not to puke, to run or to let the sensation that my heart might give out travel its course and find its deadly conclusion, but I was here and I was going to save them. All of them.

FEATURE

The rules were accepted. A Mexican wave of silent, nodding agreement swept over the room accompanied by a lot of pocket patting which I could only presume related to them all having whatever was necessary to 'pay for me'.

The next time someone spoke I was shocked by his absence as it wasn't Sutcliffe. A younger voice talked, softer, but with a similar directness. A protégé perhaps? Someone stupid enough to want to be schooled in the horrors of The Venari.

"We will now move on to the audio visual portion of the auction. There will be some footage to view, before we progress to some demonstrations of what is on offer."

The discussion of me like some piece of meat prompted a swift turn but I was unable to move enough and all I achieved was a distinct feeling of whiplash. Air hissed through my teeth and I caught the eye of a buyer on the front row, his eyes wide with anticipation. I leapt forward mockingly and reveled in the swift change from confident to petrified. It was an interesting and worthwhile experiment to find out what they really thought of me. On sight of my snigger, my minders edged closer and the one to my left nodded towards his left hand where a cattle prod slid down from his sleeve and into his waiting palm as if by magic, how ironic. I looked away and the smirk faded as I resumed my role as the clueless, helpless target. They stepped back into position but their eyes remained fixed on me, boring into my temples.

The lights dimmed and the whole room shifted within their seats. The screens must have been suspended behind me because everyone's gaze was fixed on the glow that crept into my vision from either side.

Colored haze swirled within the darkened room and I could see the colors reflected in the eyes of the audience. There were lots of muffled sounds, scuffs and thuds like an amateur home movie. I tried and failed again to twist but it was too damned uncomfortable.

The sounds started to clear and if it was possible I had audio déjà vu… these things I could hear, I had heard them before, maybe in a dream or a vision, but I knew them. I heard Sutcliffe's voice and for a second my brain was too confused to work it out and it happened slowly like cogs whirring in a machine. It was Sutcliffe talking to me.

I was forced to relive my experience in Paris in graphic detail. He had been filming the whole thing, hardly surprising but it felt strangely more invasive than I would have expected. Suppose after what happened to Edward, his penchant for footage should have been clear. I winced at the memory of the blood and his limp body alone on that wooden floor.

The time before I burned off the shackles seemed to be the longest ever. I had blocked out the memories, I guess. Then when it happened the room was flooded with a huge white light from the blast and there was a collective gasp which led to a whole new round of staring. I sensed my value had just gone up.

I felt my pulse soar at the memory of him touring the house with Mom in it, taunting me with her like someone teasing a dog with a bone and it was hell not giving in. I hadn't forgotten what was said in the van on the way here, I just had to hope it was a bluff and, if it wasn't, use it as more ammunition to ensure I succeeded. Mom, Jake, Alice, Elias... my new mantra was just a roll call of people I cared about that I had to save.

Hearing myself scream, the sounds that left my throat were primal and surprise tears pricked my eyes. I breathed deeply until they retreated. I was taken aback by how difficult I found it reliving those moments and how suddenly close to the surface those emotions and sensations felt. I could almost smell the burning flesh and keeping the memory of the pain away was like trying to ignore things crawling beneath my skin. It itched and ached and my gut writhed at the thought of that room, the strain to escape and the pure terror of being trapped in that space, with them.

I shouldn't have been surprised, but it was the sheer inhumanity of it, the constant plunging to new depths of it all; amidst their faces there were many creeping, leering smiles. The taste for what I could do was literally exciting them and my disgust was a worrying catalyst. Every time my heart beat pushed higher and the blood pumped that little bit harder, I could feel it. The tide of power was swirling and building and all I could think about was that it felt like I had swallowed a storm. Pressure built in my head and it was starting to drain me just to fight it off. I thought about it, letting go now, ending it all but there was just a small part of me that felt like it wasn't all aligned and that this whole scenario relied on the perfect timing. To end this, I had to feel at my strongest and catch them at a time they least expected it. One thing was for sure: they had already made the mistake of forgetting me. I mean, not literally, the whole thing was about me, but they were so caught up in their role play mind games about what they were doing, how they may harness me, use me, that they were overlooking the danger in front of them. I was a live grenade from which they had pulled the pin months ago.

The lights continued to flash and I disappeared inside my mind, desperately seeking to drown out the sound of my own screams. I opened them when the light stopped pulsing through my eyelids. All eyes returned to the direction of the other voice, it was the younger one again and the longer I didn't know where Sutcliffe was, the more uneasy I felt.

"So. We promise a, shall we say, comprehensive display of what is on offer. We know that you don't want to part too easily with the kind of currency we are talking about today. With that in mind we have devised a little demonstration to 'really' bring it to life for you and help reassure any of those who are not yet sure that this is one bargaining chip you really want." He lingered on the 'really' in a way that got my back up further. I didn't like any of this but I knew them and this wasn't good. From nowhere the two gargoyles assigned as my minders released me from my plastic tube and dragged me into the room to a series of appreciative 'ahhh's. Finally free to turn, I flashed my head around to beyond the cage and I got my first glimpse of him. He looked the same mostly, maybe a bit sicklier than before; perhaps my little escape had caused him some discomfort with his currently admiring audience. I bet there was more than a little unrest when he revealed he had 'lost' the prize. If these were the type of people to pay for my life and invoke me as some kind of warhead, then they wouldn't hesitate in getting to him if they felt wronged. He wouldn't be much of a target: pale and gangly, a barely there person with, what could only be, the most meager of strength.

Inevitably they moved me from one spot only to thrust me into another uncomfortable restraint. I opened my mouth but Sutcliffe closed it for me before I could speak. He moved down from his podium and his large, imposing chair towards me. His movement was arachnid in nature, unnaturally long limbs extending in multiple directions.

He approached and maneuvered himself close to me, but not so close that I could extend my chained arms to choke him as I wished to. He spoke softly so the room could still hear enough but so I knew this was all for me.

"I will remind you, Miss Roth, that we can make you do what we want and the end result of today's little... experiment can be relatively peaceful. But know this, if you should choose not to play the game, I can and will obliterate everyone and everything you have ever cared about. You will still be ours, but you will be ours and will know that nothing else exists that matters to you, anywhere. So comply or watch her die."

The sound of a door opening didn't quite register at first; I was working all his words around in my mind. When it slammed shut, I was back in the room and so was she. My heart dropped and I felt the heat of all my swallowed emotions rising once more. She was shaking and crying and her face was stained with the tracks of tears cried much before this. She reached for me and another one of the Sanguinaries batted down her hand as she winced at the blow. I couldn't hold back my involuntary heaving. I was so sure I would be sick. I had been trying so hard to convince myself this wasn't what they meant yet I had known since that moment in the van that it was but I was so bloody minded, so focused on this cause, that I didn't allow it to really penetrate my thoughts. I couldn't. But there she was.

"Mom." It was a cry that said so much more. It was a thousand apologies, an 'I love you', a 'help me', an 'I need you'. The list went on. Suddenly I was five and crying for my mom to save me from the bullies. Her face broke, her bottom lip quivered with the threat of consuming tears and then from nowhere she summoned composure. She spoke quietly and directly to me from her position just two, three feet away. They had put her as close as possible to serve as the most poignant reminder of their threat.

"Scarlett, darling. My baby. I am so sorry. Don't you dare give in for me. Don't you do it, Scarlett."

"Mom." I repeated myself for lack of all other words. Again, it said so much.

"Shh. Just…" She trailed off and for the first time in a long time, she looked at me like she really knew me again, like the Washington days and she made me realize that she got it, she understood what I was doing.

"Save them. Everyone." She knew my job here was bigger than the two of us and the fear that seeing her had struck in me waned for pride and a certain type of courage you can only get from people you love and who love you in return. I glanced to Sutcliffe, who was shifting marginally uncomfortably in his mock throne. He didn't like this, he had been expecting more of a scene, an outpouring of panic. We were more composed than he thought we would be and it had him worried.

I thought about what she said, I stared at her tired face robbed of color and I battled the constant to and fro of my imagination; what they would do to her if I got it wrong versus what could happen to her even if I got it all right.

Sutcliffe approached me once more but this time he was focused on his buyers, his mind had turned to money and theirs to domination.

"I am going to ask Miss Roth to demonstrate her skills for you. As we mentioned in your delegate documentation, these skills are very much in their infancy, but you have the categorical proof that she is the one they spoke of, we know there is more. This will be up to you to determine the value and decide what today's investment could be worth tomorrow."

My thoughts turned to Mom, there was no doubt now that she knew what had happened in Salem and I had guessed they took great delight in sharing with her the details of my capture in Paris. How must that have felt for her, learning all this from them, that way? My throat ached with sadness that I had no choice but to swallow. Save it. Use it. It was my mantra. But, even knowing she was clued in was painful and the idea of showing her exactly how much I had changed felt weird. Would she be proud that I had taken this on? Or would she wonder where her little girl had gone and wish I had kept out of it? I had been over and over it so many times, I knew that this set of events was not something I could have avoided, but maybe I could have handled it better. My approach had left people dead, people, plural and after today, well, what then? I wasn't the kind of person that was ok with a body count.

Sutcliffe moved toward me and my mom fought instinctively in her chair, twisting her limbs against their restraints. She kept calling my name. My pulse raced. Save it. Use it. I couldn't look at her, it was near impossible to hold it all in when I saw the fear in her eyes. It was pure helplessness; she knew there was nothing she could do to help me. I had seen it before, from Jake. Oh God, Jake.

I had restrained myself so long and kept Alice and Elias out to make sure I got here without hurting anyone else, but it was time to start taking control, subtly. First, I needed to know he was ok.

I closed my eyes and Sutcliffe's voice was in proximity.

He was warming them up, the crowd. Spinning them tales of my capabilities and it was almost humorous, hearing him talk about me like he was so sure, like he knew so well what I could do. Alice has once again done me proud, he was no wiser. Any concerns I had about his knowledge of me were unfounded, he was clueless.

TRAILER

He moved closer still and I knew I didn't have much time; my full presence would soon be required to secure his big financial bonus.

I drowned out the sounds of hushed conversations and Sutcliffe's tall tales and focused my mind. *Elias! Elias!* I screamed his name within the confines of my mind and it echoed back at me like I was stood on a precipice with nothing below. Please, please be ok and please help me.

There was just emptiness and dark space. It was getting harder to drown Sutcliffe out and Elias wasn't showing. *Please, Elias. Are you ok?*

My heart sank; I was almost out of time and nothing. Then, without the usual radio tune in, I sense him. I still couldn't hear anything but I knew he was listening to me, I could feel it. *Elias, I know you can hear me. Are you ok?* I heard him answer but the sound was so weak it was like he was talking through a wall of cotton wool. Was that yes?

Yes. Thank God. He was alive and ok.

I need you to check on Jake. Listen for him, make sure he is far away and safe. Can you do that? There was a faint sound but I couldn't make it out and then the connection went. Still silent but I knew he was gone and I didn't get my answer. "Goddammit, Elias, why this time, why now?"

I felt sick and the palms of my hands had started to become clammy as the tension built up in the room around me. It was coming to it, the start of the end and my emotions were so mixed I could barely breathe. It was the most accurate representation I had ever known of the pleasure, pain principle. Half of the cells in my body were alive with an electric desire to start it all and the other half were trembling with the kind of fear and trepidation barely articulable; beyond emotions and sensations it was like being possessed by fear itself, a single entity born of horror and destined to serve it to the unlucky.

I opened my eyes and drew on my fear to power me through it. Sutcliffe was crouching to meet my face with his. I turned my cheek and he grabbed me in that way he had in the asylum.

"Now. I think we start small, don't you, Miss Roth?" I turned the opposite way and twisted free of his grip. As he spoke one of the Sanguinaries wheeled through a table from the door they had brought Mom through just moments before. It was draped in a white sheet that was raised and mottled with the pull of objects below.

"On this table we have a variety of things. When I make a command, you follow." He bent down to my ear and spoke so his audience wouldn't hear his venom. "If I ask you something and you don't respond I will remove a finger from your mother's hand for every second of your disobedience." He grinned through his speech and pushed my face to meet my mother's gaze before tilting my head ever so gently with his hand to see one of the Sanguinaries to my right flash a lick of silver my way. It was a blade, four, maybe five inches long and the edge looked so sharp as it glinted reflections of the unnatural light of this place. When my eyes flashed back to Mom, she was weeping and looking down at her tied hands. I wanted to weep with her but I couldn't. A solitary tear crawled down my cheek and he caught it with his disgusting finger.

"So, we understand each other?" His eyes bore into mine and I nodded in silence. Play the game, go along with it for now.

"So, ladies and gentleman. This is where we start to have the real fun." With that the henchman dramatically removed the white sheet to display a table full of random objects. A glass of water, a metal chain coiled like a snake, a large padlock, what looked like a lump of coal and a huge book. It was all feeling strangely like a TV magic show; the unveiling, the showmanship of it all. I was amazed these people were happy to go along with such a charade if all they wanted was their chance to rule the world. Though, I suppose that was the point. They were so blinded by greed and a lust for the win that they weren't even bothered how much they were played or patronized in the build-up.

The two Sanguinaries that had been flanking me all day stepped forward and took an arm each. They pulled me to my feet and led me to the table, so it was all that stood between them and me.

"Miss Roth, we would like you to start by selecting an object at random and using your particular gifts to paint a picture for our distinguished guests." He held his gaze on me, he was nervous but trying to hide it. He was on the block too and he knew I knew it.

I stared at the table and the glass of water just called to me. Hands still shackled, I focused on it intently and tried to clear my mind, but it was almost impossible when I had no idea if Jake was safe, where Elias was and while I was facing the thought of them brutalizing my mother as she wept for her baby.

It was France all over again; the house, the late night experiments only this time I barely had to concentrate. After what had happened with The Collective using my powers to move a glass was laughable.

Every eye in the room was on that glass, including my mom's. It started to tremble and a hushed gasp rolled around the room like it was echoing. I syphoned off the tiniest amount of energy I could; I was edging close to a precipice and I couldn't undo it if I went too far. I exhaled as slowly as possible and allowed the electricity surge of energy move forward to my hands. They were shaking ever so slightly, not so anyone would notice but enough. The glass maintained its small movements and Sutcliffe took a step forward. I didn't have to look to catch the glint of the blade again. With a clenched jaw I put all my energy into the glass, but the distraction of them having my mom was proving too much. A wave of repressed rage again consumed me and with the slightest flick of my wrist the glass rose from the table; bodies started rising from their seats for a better view and the dull murmur of voices became a constant drone.

I stopped the glass just below chest height and pushed it further away from me. I saw from the corner of my eye, my mom raise her hands to her mouth; she might have been told, but pretty sure there is no substitute for seeing this first hand. I held it there for a moment and reveled in their dumb, expectant, eager faces before closing my eyes with a silent command and obliterating it with the connection of one synapse to another.

That moment was almost frozen to me. I remembered

this happening before on occasion, time slowing when my powers were in swing but this was almost like I willed it, I wanted to observe every second.

In stop motion I saw the initial separation, and then the shards of glass started to disperse in outward ripples, inching slowly away until gravity sucked them in and dragged them down like a shower of needles over the vying public. There were some startled groans and gasps punctuated with a wave of pained screams. Four or five of them in the drop zone were clutching their faces, splintered with glass. Spurred on by my own bravery or maybe idiocy I decided to couple it with another message. The Sanguinaries flexed their muscle and taunted me with the shining blade and its proximity to my mother's throat. I concentrated on the tip of the blade and found myself embroiled in a quasi-arm and mind wrestle with the one in control of it. He grunted and moaned in discomfort as I disabled his strength, the blade moving closer to his throat. The man to his right raised the alarm with a panicked cry and desperately tried to pull the arm down but gravity wasn't on his side and I wasn't about to make it easy for them. I pulled back his tense, coiled arm like a slingshot and fired the blade towards the crowd. It embedded itself firmly in the ground at the feet of two front row bidders who gasped in unison. The Sanguinaries dropped their guard very briefly, but I caught those worried glances

As if from nowhere, Sanguinaries appeared and escorted

them out of the room for medical attention, I presumed. Sutcliffe was in my face before I could blink and he hissed through gritted teeth.

"I said no games. Anything else like this happens here today and she will be repatriated in a series of tiny boxes." He nodded at my mother, who was still weeping silently. Meanwhile the incessant chatter was gaining volume fast as anxiety mixed with excitement spread. Some of them were worryingly unperturbed and practically hopped up and down in their places chanting 'more, more'. It felt a bit like the most disturbing kids' party of all time and I was the weirdo clown performing the tricks.

"We apologize for any concern, as we stressed these abilities are in their infancy and can be tamed over time. Please do not be concerned, we have the situation in hand." He stared at me with cold eyes and mouthed 'next'.

I searched what was left and my eyes just stopped at the padlock; maybe it was symbolic or just that it was heavy and the temptation was great to use it to knock out my minders and get the hell out of that room.

It was almost instant; the rise in my blood pressure remained from the glass incident and I was feeling the strongest desire to surrender to my potential. I had goose pimples the length of my arms and the slideshow of images in my mind did nothing to diffuse the bomb ticking within me. Jake. Alice. Elias.

My right hand hovered over the lock and a sensation of

warmth immediately spread and filled the air between. It was just a split second before warm turned to heat and if I wasn't in the headspace of my powers I would have had to move but instead I kind of thought over it, talked myself around the pain. I breathed slowly and with purpose, focusing all my will on the energy from my hands. It was like I could feel every molecule and atom. The air vibrated and shook as if it were scared of what was coming. Maybe I was too.

A small swirl of gray smoke streamed upwards from the metal and, for a second, I was the only one who saw it. But as it rose heads turned and interest peaked in what was happening. The gray surface blurred as a haze of orange and red engulfed it. Within what could not have been more than about ten seconds the whole thing was alive with white hot heat and its form loosened slowly at first, then all at once it kind of collapsed. The once solid metal oozed and inched its way across the table in a rivulet of molten liquid. The smell of burning spread throughout the room as the table was scorched and the heat of the metal sank into the weakened wood.

Sutcliffe stepped forward and smiled at his public before nodding to start a sweep of slow clapping. There was lots of appreciative nodding, the buyers were pleased it seemed. Sutcliffe shot me a weird semi-smile, like he was congratulating me on a job well done. I looked away and realized I couldn't keep doing this; this pretense was going to have to end and I needed to activate my plan sooner or later. I doubted myself and it wasn't safe to do that and I knew it. I had to start making some choices. I was starting to regret my rashness and wishing I had bought myself that bit more time, that The Collective hadn't left so soon and I had been able to work on all this that bit more. Even I was sick of my own yo-yoing confidence. I just needed that push and I needed it soon.

Sutcliffe gestured to the Sanguinaries, who appeared alongside me instantly and swept the table away as suddenly as it had arrived. I was confused, why take it away now when there was more to show?

A hand from behind pulled me back into a waiting chair.

"Wait. What are you...?" The words were abruptly halted before I could finish. My mouth was taped and I struggled against the pressure being applied to my arms; they were being strapped down. My mom started calling out, just saying my name over and pleading for them to stop. Sutcliffe had some guy in a white coat I hadn't seen before stick electrodes on my temples and my chest.

"We have learnt from our other interactions with Miss Roth that emotional stimuli are most effective in drawing out her potential." He nodded to one of my minders, who was now positioned by the door. The waiting man received the nod and swung the door open. Another person backed in slowly and it took me a moment to realize they were pulling something. Not something, someone. A wheelchair.

I strained my neck to try to see who it was and I couldn't move far enough without cutting myself against the restraints. They were pushing all the right buttons though and they knew it. Sutcliffe didn't take his eyes off me the whole time.

A voice in my head screamed *You can tear out of this now… do it. Run.* But I couldn't place it or work out how. I had been so careful to close myself off, keep this private between me and them but somehow someone was in. My mind was clouded with confusion and the pressure to pick my moment. It was so obvious and I should have known they would do it but my mind was too busy to think as logically as that. It couldn't be.

The mysterious driver spun round and the air was immediately sucked from my lungs. The person in front of me was a shadow of the one I remembered and it felt like the time that had lapsed was more like years. His faced was older and angry purple bruising mottled his skin which was gray and tired. His hair fell limply and the lack of light and strength in him was suffocating. The air had left my lungs and wasn't coming back. I gasped in panic behind my gag and hands pulled me down against the chair. I kept wondering if you could drown in sadness, because seeing him like that made it feel possible.

Elias stood before me, his hands on the wheelchair and I couldn't take my eyes off him even though I was barely able to see for the tears filling them. This was out of control. He stared at me and cut through the emotion in my mind with the saddest, most painful words I could have imagined, *I tried*, as he looked down.

His knuckles were bloody and raw, he had been pushed to the edge and kept himself to himself this whole time to spare me. It didn't make sense though; why bring him in now?

In all the commotion I had not even acknowledged his role in the charade or who they had him wheel in. I wasn't in the shape I needed to be and what I saw next did nothing to improve my state of mind. They had gone all out; whatever they were hoping to achieve they wanted something big. If emotion was their weapon they were going big.

I should have known instantly, it made perfect sense for it to be her and she was as broken as I had worried. My visions of her were sadly accurate. Her chest heaved slowly and her eyes remained closed in a lolling head that fell toward her chest. Alice.

I fought against my gag and pulled my hands. The black space inside me that once meant fear now meant something else. It was power and a desire to prove a point and make so many things right. Starting today. If my confidence were to be this roller-coaster I was getting to the top right now. These people I cared about in one room, it meant something, that I had no choice but to win, that had to be the legacy from this experience. I selfishly found time in all the chaos to thank God that it wasn't Jake pulling that chair but I wasn't stupid enough to not be concerned by it either. Maybe they thought this was enough, maybe they knew once I was here I would fight to save anyone I cared about?

Alice was nearing the end, clinging by snapped nails to the life she had surrendered for my cause years before. The only small comfort I could think of was that for this last tiny part of what had been a torturous journey, she had been in the company of someone good. Elias was many things, but he would have reminded her what kindness was and his compassion would have been enough to show her humanity was not dead. No-one should leave this world thinking that all that won over was evil, there had to be some light to carry her through. He would have given that to her.

I could hear her labored breathing and it made me think of my own; keep going, breathe, not yet.

The silence had endured long enough and Sutcliffe was pleased enough with my response to his little experiment. It was written all over his vile, motionless face. This had been a bit too easy, too civilized so far, for them at least. I shouldn't have been even remotely surprised to find myself at this particular juncture; I knew they would seek leverage and I suppose I had just been too focused on my role to think of what that might have meant. This was becoming my problem; I was trying to see everything and as a result was seeing nothing. I had been lost in another of my inner monologues and what the audience had been doing had fallen off my radar, that was until I saw some people at the back rising for what I assumed was a desire to gain a better view. But as their eyes met mine and moved on, then scanned Elias and Alice's and still passed by, I realized it wasn't us they were interested in, it was something else. They were looking beyond me, back to the screen and Sutcliffe was joining them. His dead expression slowly gave way to one of his creeping smirks and so I contorted my neck, feeling the hot burn of tightening skin as I craned to see.

Where the video had been playing previously was now an erratic performance of angry lines dancing into ever increasing peaks and troughs. He was showing them what happened to me when he threatened people I cared about. As the anger I was feeling bounced from nerve to nerve throughout my shaking body, the screen lit up with activity. More bodies rose from their seats as I started to struggle against my restraints. I was beginning to fall to the urge to fight; my idea of keeping it all in was a losing battle. A myriad of sensations passed through me, it was like being electrocuted, losing gravity, as if I was watching myself from the outside. The ground below my chair quaked and, without looking at the screen, their faces told me what was happening. It was off the charts.

Elias pulled back, he knew well enough and he dragged Alice with him. He stood in front of her and protectively shielded her from the perceived threat. He didn't know what was going to happen, but he knew that was half the problem; my powers to this point had always felt a bit like a lucky dip to bystanders and he had been privy to more than most.

Elias, I don't feel like I can hold it back anymore, but I don't want to hurt you and Alice and my mom. Help me. I looked at him for a second and the briefest flash of light showed in his eyes. *Yes you can, you have this, Scarlett. You can do whatever you want and you can control this. You showed that in Amsterdam, hell, even in Paris. Focus.*

With that, he looked away and centered his gaze on my mom. He pulled Alice towards her and stood with them both behind his back. The Sanguinaries were too focused on the fuss my mind was creating on the screen and on the increasing excited chatter from their distinguished guest.

I was all but surrendered, my mind almost lost to the sensation of falling, when a voice from the crowd slammed on the brakes.

A tall, thin man with olive skin and a well-cut blue suit rose to his feet. He passed a hand over his slicked back hair and cleared his throat before starting to speak.

"I have seen enough. It is clear that Miss Roth has the abilities of which you have spoken and I think I can speak for all interested parties when I say there is no need for further delay. Let us start the bidding." A raucous cheer passed through the seated section of the room. His English was weighted with a heavy accent, but he was well spoken and I wanted to scream at the top of my lungs, I am a person, a human, what is wrong with you? But, there were no words in my throat, just an ache and the ember of the rage from the moments before.

Several others rose to their feet and Sutcliffe turned to face them, a hint of fluster to his stance. He looked like it may have dawned on him that these were hungry lions, possibly even more motivated by greed than he was by hate and that was a powerful mix; he couldn't keep 'showing' them, he needed to deliver and they were not as pliable as he had hoped. They were going to be calling the shots and he was going to have to surrender to that.

It was kind of fascinating, watching him be manipulated and coerced this way, to see him as the weaker one. They were likely to turn on him if he didn't give them what they wanted and, if it hadn't been me, I would probably have enjoyed the 'turning of tables' element of this scenario.

Sutcliffe stepped up to regain control. He nervously brushed down his jacket and wrung his hands. "Our guest is quite right. We had planned to show you more, but, as you can see, our subject's brain activity is far beyond that which many of us have ever seen. Miss Roth can be trained, tested, her mind expanded and her gifts exploited. We know many of you have exciting plans for someone of her ability and we are excited to present this opportunity for you."

The audience was now almost totally on its feet. The

Sanguinaries had resumed security detail, separating Sutcliffe from the crowd, due to a definite air of unrest.

"May I remind you all, before we begin, that Miss Roth is unlike any of the subjects we have seen before." My mind stopped whirring for a moment to process that there had been more of me.

"She has long foretold capabilities much beyond anything we have seen here today. So please, bear this in mind when we start our bidding."

The young guy who had done much of the speaking at the beginning stepped forward. He was small and mousy and didn't look the sort. Which seemed a stupid thing to even think, knowing now that there really wasn't 'a sort' but he looked just so normal and nerdy and, well, soft. He looked like, well, like I would probably have been friends with him if I was doing normal things like going to college and making friends that didn't know me because they, too, had supernatural powers.

"May I remind you all of the regulations set out at the start of today's meeting. These will be upheld and anyone not willing to adhere will be asked to leave and their bids will be void."

He stepped forward to command attention and the room brightened as extra lights were switched on for the big show. After all this, it was a simple battle between greed and hatred, I was kind of incidental; you could have substituted me for a magic lamp or a rune stone that could predict the future. The flutter of a butterfly's wings hundreds of years ago could have started all of this and I would never know why me, but today I was fulfilling a prophecy, I was being 'The One' and it was the strangest feeling in the world. I cast my eyes to Alice; this broken, lifeless woman whose own life had been surrendered by a desire to assist me in mine and I felt a surge of love. She was remarkable. She could have walked away, she didn't need to leave the trail and endanger herself the way she did and her selflessness was the only reason I had the chance to prepare. If they had managed to snatch me before I started learning through her words, there is no telling what would have become of me by this point; well, I suppose history held some worrying clues.

Sutcliffe let his minion take charge and a tangible air of excitement once again filled the room. The smell of smoke had gone and was replaced with the heat of multiple bodies sweating through anxious waiting. I felt sick; it was the smell and it was my own personal brand of anxiety, its name was 'eradicate only the bad ones, make the right choices, timing is everything', catchy.

"Ok. Let's get this started. Remember what we are bidding for please, ladies and gentlemen. We are not haggling and we start our bid at three million Euros." He paused and I caught Elias's expression. He was almost himself for a moment; there was a smug smirk like he was laughing about my 'worth'.

Bizarrely no one blinked and as I studied some of the faces in the crowd I saw subtle hints of humor, like they too thought it was laughable, but their reaction was different to Elias's. They weren't laughing because it was an extortionate amount of money, they were laughing because they thought it was cheap.

In the seconds that filled the void, a sea of hands shot up and voices started jostling for position in the humid air. The next few minutes passed in a blur. Voices were calling out over and above each other, it quickly deteriorated into something more resembling a meat market than the highbrow bidding system I know Sutcliffe was hoping for.

The Sanguinaries hushed the crowd and pushed some of the more eager front row bidders back to their seats. The amount climbed every split second and we were already at eight. Sutcliffe stepped to the fore again and hushed the crowd with an extension of his bony hand towards the room. They, like obedient children this time, silenced. Now the money was on the table they were willing to pay attention.

"Now, now. Remember what we are offering here, please. This opportunity supersedes bombs and guns, biological warfare. We have seen people much less powerful than her read minds, for Christ's sake; she can probably even control them. So let's bid like we mean it shall we? Take it to ten, will you."

FEATURE

Twelve. Thirteen. Sixteen. Then a voice at the back boomed above them all as a figure rose from his seat and pursed his lips assertively.

"Stop this game. Why are we pretending with such amounts? Let us do as he said and make this real." He stepped out of his row and started a slow, confident saunter down the aisle towards the center where I was being kept. The Sanguinaries stood to attention aware of the potential for subtle change in the balance of power. They sought approval from Sutcliffe to shut the situation down; after all, this man was not supposed to be walking around and calling the shots.

As he moved closer Sutcliffe motioned for the muscle to stand down. They were like dogs; rabid and vicious, but they loved their master. They relaxed their hunched shoulders enough to go from menacing to averagely intimidating.

Our mystery man paced forward. He wore a dark gray suit with a light gray shirt, no tie. He was clean shaven and slightly younger than the average age of the demographic. His face was softer, less 'battle hardened' but he wore his expression with such conviction, I wouldn't have taken him on in a fight. You could tell he was articulate and confident in this situation.

Sutcliffe braced his shoulders and stepped towards the front to greet this leader among the room of followers. Sutcliffe liked people who stood out when the reasons were right and, let's face it, he could only win. If more money was on the table, he was the one that would get to pocket it.

When our new fearless bidder reached the front he walked towards me and knelt before my chair. My pulse thumped in my head and I tried nervously to avoid his gaze, but it was to no avail. He placed his hands on my cheeks and pulled my face.

He had the darkest eyes I had ever seen. They were brown but encircled by an almost black hoop. I don't think anyone had ever seen anything like it. He made a point of holding my gaze and I felt a strange sensation pass through me. It wasn't until I cleared my mind of everything else just for second that I worked it out. The feeling I was having was a fleeting flash of recognition. It wasn't blurry and dreamy like déjà vu... it was real.

He saw the moment as it passed behind my eyes but he didn't react; there was just an air of understanding. I wasn't sure what I was feeling. It didn't register as fear. I wasn't scared of him exactly, I was on edge. Wary because I couldn't place him and it was unnerving. Then there was a feeling of falling, intense and stomach jerking free-fall. I felt like I wasn't recalling a memory so much as being sucked straight through time to relive it. It felt like the ground was slowly falling away from me.

I was taking those tentative steps towards the gate and the throng of people and looking at those faces. My mind reviewed the sight for me and the retrospective was illuminated somehow, like I was seeing with fresh eyes through a macro lens. Every detail stood out, fibers of their clothes, the smell on the breeze, the sensation of every hair on my arm standing on end as I edged closer, battling my trepidation. In the slow motion replay I was cautious, attentive and then thud; it hit me. He was there, waiting, watching intently. He was from The Collective.

I gasped louder than I had intended and it drew unwanted attention. He was close to my face but remained motionless and silent. When the sound had all escaped and only my heightened pulse and breathing could be felt between us he rose again without a word.

He wasn't one of the ones that came in, I definitely never interacted with him but he was there and now he was here. My mind ran wild. Why was he here? Surely if he was here to help he wouldn't be drawing such attention to himself; I mean, he couldn't have been less conspicuous if he had sledged hammered his way through the dry wall. The whole room was focused on him and now the pair of us together. My brain twitched and hissed with possibility to communicate and I guessed it was Elias offering his thoughts. He will sure as hell have heard the noise of that flashback and he wasn't one to hold back on his theories, good or bad. I shot him a glance but he was looking at Alice, one hand resting on hers and with the other he swept her hair away from her eyes which remained closed. It wasn't him, he wasn't speaking to me.

Our mystery man strode confidently to the front of the audience, practically cozying up with the Sanguinaries like he was the most perfect fit in the world, the bidder they had all been waiting for and it confused me further. Was he a mole then, back in Amsterdam? Is that how they found me? It would make sense looking at Alice, but then, maybe the game starts here and he is on my side? This was bull and I was getting twitchy. Every little query or concern sent my blood pressure up a notch and the window was closing for me to play the game. If I didn't keep it in control now it may be too dangerous even for me to let go.

He spoke. "I want to make this the auction it was meant to be. She is The One. This foretold prophecy dates hundreds of years. We have all waited years for the chance to own power like this. There is no substitute. Scarlett Roth is the most dangerous and powerful weapon any one of us has ever known. I have seen it." There were a series of confused and agitated sounds from the others. They didn't like his stance and they didn't like his claim to have had intel. Nor did I.

"I have been witness to other gifts, ones even our clueless hosts The Venari were unable to extricate and to which they continue to be blind." If he knew, really knew what I could do he was selling me out. To what end I had no idea but I sensed the very rapid decline of the situation and my gut reaction was to let it go now, to just be this person they wanted me to be.

The Sanguinaries tensed at the insult and Sutcliffe took a step forward as he nodded at them to keep their distance. Our mystery stranger turned to face Sutcliffe and smirked.

"You have us here, playing your hand like you're winning but you are running scared. You don't know exactly what it is your little lab rat can do. Oh I know you know it's big; your little informant…" he gestured to Alice who was still slumped in the chair, her raspy breathing the only sound as the conversation broke down…" she wasn't wrong. Miss Roth is The One your organisation has been looking for all these years, but the scale of what you are dealing with here? You have no idea."

Sutcliffe was tense. It was etched in the bristly, sinewy muscles in his jaw as he attempted to hide his increasing concern for the manner in which this stranger was draining his power.

"I know, I know. You've run your tests and you've tortured the truth from your little second class witch over there. Congratulations, you are still on the back foot." The atmosphere was changing, colder now and a room of eagerness had shifted to discomfort and anxiety. The other bidders lost their gall. It somewhat altered the dynamic when those who were running the show were being so spectacularly trumped.

"Mr…?" Sutcliffe was using his professional voice now. I had heard it before, in the Asylum.

"Van Ives." The stranger purred back, so clearly delighted with the attention.

"Well, Mr Van Ives. We may not know all that she is capable of but never did we promise anything to the contrary, In fact, today, here in this very room, we confessed that these bids were speculative. We don't have all the answers, but we know they are there. So perhaps we should be focusing on the bidding. I believe you were saying something about making real bids? So, please… proceed with your offer or kindly be seated." By this point our friendly neighborhood thugs were squared up in an overt display of testosterone in action. This was now a pissing contest and The Venari intended to lay claim to its territory.

"I thought better of you, Dr Sutcliffe. I thought you were smart and logical. If she is as powerful as you claim, then why on earth is she still sitting there, shackled to that chair? She would surely have utilized this power to escape. Yes? Of course she would. She is there because she is capable and she is waiting. Like I said. I have seen this in action and you are playing with fire."

I was flushed with heat and rage. Who was this Van Ives and why the hell was he selling me out? He was taking away the impact of all of this time sent harboring stupid, heavy secrets and practicing; all the endless trials to focus and build strength.

"Mr Van Ives." He raised his voice and his dogs took a step forward. "Please make your bid or leave." Sutcliffe was nervous. It was written all over his face as he to-ed and fro-ed over whether to look at Van Ives for what he might do next, or me, the loose cannon, if our guest was to be believed.

The almost stranger took a breath and extended his fingers in front of him before proceeding to crack his knuckles loudly. "Fine. Ignore my warnings... but..." the words were formed in his mouth but not yet released when the ripple of unrest was unleashed. It started with quizzical glances and quickly escalated into row upon row of bodies abandoning their seats, taking to their feet. There was a cacophony of shouts and abuse towards Sutcliffe. They wanted to know if it was safe to be in this room, if the proper procedures were in place to keep me at bay. They weren't.

Sanguinaries were radioed in from the halls and built a defensive barrier at the front of the room, which by this point had a definite air of pre-riot about it. Angry foreign languages were being hurled around, amongst themselves and at a progressively weary looking Sutcliffe. He had not anticipated any kind of issue at all. Our Venari intern took to the microphone to try to settle things down, which did nothing to dissuade our concerned guests.

A commotion broke out about four rows back. Someone threw a punch and it was suddenly like having front row seats to the spread of a rage in a zombie movie. The little concerned chatter and questions turned to accusatory, jealous jibes and once that first fist made contact with a stranger's skin, all was lost. All excitement had been replaced with aggravated tension. They all wanted me so badly but not one of them had considered the implications of securing the power they all so desperately sought.

Van Ives stood, arms folded and completely failing to conceal his glee at what was unfolding. Who the hell was this person and what was he hoping to achieve?

Sanguinaries fought their way through and separated three men embroiled in a fist fight. It was then I knew I had to do something. I needed to clear some of these people out of this room in as peaceful a way as possible and under a cover that was believable. The less people around now, the less at the end when it really hit the fan. I had made as much peace as was possible with the fact that there would always be some collateral damage, but if I could reduce it by any amount maybe the karma would work out better? I knew these weren't good men, but, as yet, they had not harmed me, wronged me and I had to spare them if I could.

With my eyes wide, I fixed my gaze on the far right section of the room and did my best to keep as much in my peripheral vision as I could. I skimmed the top of the sensation hiding within me and it felt like the bit of the storm that follows you in through a door. A hint of something bigger and much more powerful beyond.

I remembered Amsterdam and my mind filled with thoughts of that house, the smells, of Jake, of my letters to those I love but to whom I might never say goodbye. I thought of their faces, the blood that ran within their veins, forever etched with words we spoke together, moments we shared and how these people in this room wanted to take me away from all that. Suddenly it was easy.

The air ran cold around me and I remained fixed on them. This was one of the ones I didn't feel like I had practiced enough; largely because it felt like such a gross invasion of human rights. Taking control of people was wrong, but I wasn't planning to hurt them; if anything, I was saving them. Whether the benefit was long term would remain to be seen. It was potentially another blood on my hands situation, but right now, it was time. The rest would have to wait.

The thought was easy. Just change your mind. Realize you don't feel safe here, that this isn't what you were promised and that you think you should leave.

There was a worryingly long pause between the thought and it generating any kind of response in them. It was so subtle. I only knew it worked because I knew the look. There was a sort of lost and confused air to their faces, like they just woke up from a coma and had no idea how they ended up in that room.

Then, just like that they dropped their fists. Looked at each other and the Sanguinaries poised to 'isolate the incident' and retreated. They picked up their things, closely followed by several people either side on each row, turned around and headed to the doors at the back. My head was throbbing, the projection of thought was very draining and I was starting to panic that I was using too much juice on this. I had to convince them to leave. I pushed them harder. It was like being inside the minds of all twenty, maybe thirty of them.

They stopped and when they got to the door, I pushed harder than ever. GO. They looked to Sutcliffe who stood bewildered but in light of the chaos nodded, defeated at the henchman and they swung open the doors. The room stared on, unsure of what just happened and our compere was back, trying to regain control.

I hadn't realized I had been holding my breath the entire time. I could feel my grip slipping on their consciousness as they moved further and further away from the room, but if my experiences were anything to go by, they would be so confused they wouldn't even try to get back in. My head pounded as a result of the exertion and Elias clocked me holding my skull to try to quash the sensation.

What's happening, Scarlett?

I made them leave. I wanted to clear some people out of here and it was getting too tense. I want to keep this controlled. Little damage as possible.

Ok. Be careful though. I don't think all of these guys would give up so easy. And that guy... isn't he...?

We were cut off before he could finish his sentence. Sutcliffe clapped loud and slow. "Well, Mr Van Ives, congratulations. If your little show was to reduce the competition a little, then you succeeded. So, will you be bidding or joining them?" He had his patter back but he was shaken. I could sense it. I could probably have honed into every molecule in that room in that moment. Van Ives shot me a look and I remained puzzled by his place here. I expected him to leave, to have been a bluffing blip in the midst of this chaos, but he didn't. He pushed out his chest and stood taller than before.

"Very well. As I said. You misunderstood the worth. So I raise the bid. Twenty million Euros." There were some glances exchanged; some between bidders, the stone- faced Sanguinaries shifted just ever so slightly on their spots. He stepped nonchalantly back down into the seated area of the room and as he reached the middle of the aisle he looked back at Sutcliffe, "That is reducing the competition."

Sutcliffe knew best that he had to hold his position to retain control. He must be composed, no matter what. The change in dynamics had left an unpleasant sensation on his skin, it seeped in and I could see him squirming below the surface. He hoped to already be sipping Mojitos on a yacht by now; instead he found himself unsettlingly off balance in a room of people that wanted him out of the way to get to me. When money and blood, lust and greed met like this it was a heady combination. It was a toxic fog of emotions and heightened senses and every moment that ticked by it morphed into something more dangerous.

Van Ives sat back down in silence amidst a whispered rumble of consideration for next moves and discontent. They all had the money to outbid him and he knew it, but they were losing faith in what Sutcliffe knew and he had rattled a few cages. The room was divided between those that wanted me more than ever and those for whom the risk that I was in fact just a girl with a penchant for trickery was starting to look at little too great. I can see why. If The Venari had invented me and what I could do, beyond what little I had shown, it would be too late once they had purchased me. The Venari were the masters of invisibility and I was wholly confident, as were our bidders, that they could sneak off and disappear into the world without leaving a single trace. Where do you start looking for a thousand, million, maybe more, doctors and politicians and lawyers in a world of white coats and cheap power suits? It was nigh on impossible.

PRICE

A feverish bidding war broke out as fast as the punch up that had preceded it. The price on my head rose from a frankly ridiculous twenty million to over seventy five in less than the time it took for five hands to touch the air. Elias was open mouthed, but, more than that, he was furious. The rage was directed at me and he was screaming at me to end it. Alice was still lifeless in her chair and the slight movements in her chest were borderline undetectable at times, which caused a series of double takes to make sure she hadn't left us.

Sutcliffe started to shake off his concern and the smug

grimness which was his usual look started to creep back in. With every bid confirmed he executed a sly little nod. Every time he did it, I felt it grate on me. His very being continued to cause my skin to itch and strain my gag reflex until the urge to throw up was almost overwhelming. My mouth was swimming with saliva, which I swallowed nervously, and my skin glistened with sweat. I didn't feel good.

He moved his hands together, rubbing them gleefully and I could hear the rasp of course skin as if it were sandpaper on wood. This must be what Spiderman felt like; acute senses making it impossible to think. So much focus that it became counter-productive. The room was a cacophony of breath, the subtle drag of fabric against fabric as arms were crossed, legs tapped nervously, the wrap of feet on the floor and the painful, concealed whimpers of my mom from within the fold of Elias's arms.

Van Ives rose to his feet, arms folded and he boldly lay down another bid, far exceeding the one that had just been placed. Another man, paler skin and a light brown suit jacket and the kind of hair you need to brush out of your eyes a hundred times a day stepped up from his seat.

"It seems we still play. I say two hundred million." Heads turned and Sutcliffe smirked. The crowd shifted uncomfortably in some cases. A blond man, in an open shirt and no tie in the first row stood up. He cleared his throat and made a counter bid without so much as blinking.

Another casual fifty million. Money was nothing in this room. This was something else though. He was looking at me, which in itself was barely remarkable, I was exhibit A, but there was a definite something about the way he looked at me. Like the way Van Ives had. Unsettling and intriguing all at once. He wasn't as unnerving as his predecessor, but something was still off and the tension that existed in the room the entire time just went up a notch when they looked at me in that way.

While I was still trying to place whatever feeling it was my gut was experiencing another man rose to his feet, and then another. It didn't stop until a third of the room were upstanding, all shouting their bids at Sutcliffe, but all staring at me in the same way.

I clasped my head as my brain started to burn with activity. Sutcliffe shot me a glance, he was worried I was a little unpredictable and, with so much money on the table, he wanted to avoid a scene that may compromise him. Van Ives had shaken him and he wasn't so resolute in his belief that he was in charge; it was written in the sheen on his pallid skin, on the almost invisible tick that only I saw every time another person stood up.

I could hear the familiar fuzz, that hum of a message, but without looking at Elias I knew it wasn't him. I had gotten used to his sound, the way his brain felt when it connected with mine. This was different. It was messier, less practiced and busy. If the radio static sounds I always heard when tuning in were voices, then this was a chorus line of static. The drone of people speaking, or in this case thinking, all at the same time. I shook my head, desperately trying to free up enough space to find some clarity in the chaos. I tried to tune in my mind, focus on one signal but they were frantic, screaming sounds and I was one wavelength away from the sound being drowned out by my bleeding ears.

In my confusion I looked up for just a second to the waiting eyes of every bidder that had risen to stand. The eyes of every single one were boring into me and as soon as I looked into theirs the noise in my head intensified. Passing my gaze between them was equivalent to turning the dial on the radio. I could identify the sound that belonged to each of them and as my eyes moved over it got clearer. When my sight found Van Ives, it was finding the station after hours of white noise. Suddenly the monochrome haunting in my mind was technicolor and the scratching, monotonous sounds started to become less and less blurred.

You hear me don't you? Focus. Listen to what I am telling you. I was trying to focus, but doing that while not looking like I was a million miles away was another thing and I was acutely aware of Sutcliffe and some of the others continuing their auction.

Pay attention, he yelled. It turned out Van Ives's internal voice was more aggressive than Elias's. Well, more at stake, I guess.

Who the hell are you?

Oh, Scarlett, you still have so little faith in yourself and us?

I said, who are you? I can only guess from your bid you have your own agenda for me to follow, so you may as well just get it out there now and tell me.

No, you have me wrong. This, little charade is for their benefit, but I have no interest, intent or, indeed, funds to purchase you to any end. My role here is to help you.

Help me how?

I know you have had a rough time but, is your brain really so masked with the atrocities of these people that you have forgotten what it is to have comrades, protectors?

I have some of them already and all that has gotten them and me so far is hurt. You've been in this room all this time. Look to the front. That is Alice and my mom, both of whom are likely to die because of me. So please, don't speak to me of protection. Just answer my question.

Everyone you see before you is here to help. Your innocence and blindness has its uses, I suppose this would never have worked if you knew we were coming. We don't have much time. We have held off some of these people, but there is little they wouldn't do to have the chance to own your power. We don't have much time. If they realize who we are, we will all be killed. Whatever we want to do, we must do it and soon.

Are you... are you all from The Collective? The sound in my head finally dimmed as though my acceptance had silenced them and they were exhaling with relief. I was possibly the slowest 'gifted' person they had ever come across and my role as 'The One' was no doubt thrown into question at several junctures during this chaos. I had been so busy thinking about Mom and my role and how to play this, that I had essentially turned off my witch radar. There, I had said it. It was the first time, albeit only in my head, but it was an admission that had held me hostage, kept me constrained into an endless cycle of failing to test my potential. Making that leap, recognizing myself for what I was, well it was a surge of relief so vast it was hard to define. A witch. The words swam around in my brain where space had instantly been freed. It was like the joy of that moment when you are still awake but sleep envelopes your brain and you fall in a good way.

Yes. Once we knew what you could do, that it was true, we knew we had to wait for you to take your own path and then help in any way we could. This is it, for what it is. This is our gift to you. We cannot fight this fight for you, but we can be here and we can give you what we have, such as it is. It has always been about your discovery, about how you choose to end this. It was never for us to decide. The lore on you always detailed this as a solo mission, but with us here, you can source what you need and hopefully it is enough to make it real, to bring about the end.

So what now? I thought I was ready, but the thought of shedding blood, especially innocent blood. I don't know how to handle this.

The very idea of my actions hurting people, even violent douchebags, was enough to cause me physical pain. I didn't want to be like them, I just wanted it to stop.

Scarlett, you need to focus. I think you're right though about the hurt. We must only do what is absolutely necessary here. I think we need to reduce the numbers. I will work with my colleagues to price some of these other bidders out. Once we have the numbers down, we can focus on our friendly neighborhood psychopaths first. He flashed his eyes momentarily at the Sanguinaries, who, true to form, had not shifted an inch.

I agreed silently. We had to cut this short or we were bound to attract some unwanted attention.

I was already doing it, drawing power from them now I knew. It might have been the placebo of the confidence boost it gave me to feel like someone had my back but, whatever it was, it worked. With Elias behind me and them in front, things suddenly looked a lot less bleak. My skin buzzed with possibility and the feeling of power rising to the surface, pushing its way through my veins into every limb.

Sutcliffe cleared his throat and if I hadn't been so distracted by the sound of his claggy phlegm, I might not been so surprised when he stepped up alongside me.

His pointed fingers gripped the top of my head and abruptly turned it to the side toward him.

"Almost there." He hissed the words and glee oozed from him on his sickly breath. I held mine so as not to share the air with him and he smirked as he released me and inched towards his bodyguards at the front.

"Gentlemen, many of you seem to be so excited by this opportunity that you simply cannot be seated. I am to assume then, that you are all deathly serious about this opportunity."

Van Ives was shadowed by several other of the upstanding Collective as he nodded in agreement. Someone at the back raised their hand, another offered a casual nod and the bidding took right off again. It soared relentlessly and the money became so outlandish and ridiculous that I tuned it out. I spent some of the time looking at Mom. She had stopped crying now and it was like she knew, like she had sensed the change in dynamic. She had switched from being terrified of what they might do to me, to interested in what I might do to them. She still clung to Elias though and it was heart- warming to see more of his softer side. He was so good with people when he wasn't wrapped up in being a defensive, 'the world owes me a favor' ass.

I had lost track of how long it had been since I paid attention to the room, but something had changed. Silence had spread and people were leaving.

Sutcliffe shook hands with a man, probably in his mid-forties. Another sharp suit with not a lot to say. His skin matched the gray of his jacket and he looked tired. I empathized. That said, his desire to be largely mute didn't really bother me, he was one of the Collective and that was good enough for me. Stage one was largely complete.

Some of the others continued to file out of the doors at the back. A few of the Collective went with them, I guess to keep up appearances and avoid drawing attention. The rest loitered as long as they could but all bar three were gone. Van Ives was still present.

"Dr Sutcliffe. These are my associates. They represent the same organization as me and I will have them with me while we complete the transaction if this is agreeable."

Sutcliffe looked them over. Van Ives he knew, he didn't like, but he knew. The other two stood arms folded neatly in front of their bodies but Sutcliffe checked out his own protection and I think it was a case of mine are bigger than yours so he let it slide.

"Shall we?" He gesticulated behind me and the body to go with the young minion's voice followed. The young one motioned for Elias to stand and he and my mom were ushered towards the door.

"Where are you taking them?" Sutcliffe was basking in the concern in my voice, the glee practically radiated off him. Minion glanced back, his hand still firmly grasping Elias's arm and stared blankly. Elias yanked himself free and protectively shielded my mom who was struggling and trying to double back towards me. Her eyes were full again, tears threatening to consume her.

"Mom. It's ok. It is all ok, I promise." My voice trailed off as a lump in my throat constricted it and stopped the ends of the words from making it out. Elias nodded at me and without even our own silent conversation he had told me he was keeping my mom safe.

One of the Sanguinaries hurried them out and they were gone. The silence compared to the drone of the hundreds of voices was deafening and somehow claustrophobic, but I was still riding on the high of having some secret backup.

"Miss Roth. Meet Mr…"

"Vaughn." Mr Tired Eyes, member of the Collective, eyed me but was careful not to give anything away.

"Mr Vaughn is the winning bidder, so we will tie up what we need and you will be free to go with him." The tone of his voice was saturated in his adrenalin and triumph.

I almost had to laugh. Free. I hadn't been that since I set foot in Salem. Vaughn maintained his scripted disinterest in me and Van Ives too; they were playing the game beautifully. Still battling the sight of my mom being taken from me again, I tried to focus.

"Mr Vaughn, if you and your associates would like to follow me, we will take this discussion somewhere a little more comfortable." One of the remaining Sanguinaries took my arm and led me out first. We left the room by one of the side exits and passed briefly through another glossy looking waiting space dotted with plush chairs and passed through it with our echoing footsteps on the polished stone floor.

We took a left into a smaller room, still formal as you would expect but this was just a meeting room, I guessed. One large oval table and ten chairs. High tech video calling equipment and a flat screen TV at each end of the room. I was forced down into another seat, nothing special about this one but he clasped shut my constraints around it nonetheless. Sutcliffe filed in, followed by another minder, the Van Ives, Vaughn and their friends. We weren't looking at each other, I was playing along and looking as terrified as I remembered feeling in Salem and, again, in Paris. It was strangely easy to conjure those feelings no matter how positive I might feel, they were always right there.

They took their seats, Sutcliffe at the head of the table, obviously. He outstretched his arms and rested his hands on the table. He looked beyond me to the hall and nodded. The door which was half shut swung open and another horde of people filed in. Older, sinewy men, not so many young suits as in the room we had just left. They shared more than a few characteristics with Sutcliffe than I was happy to acknowledge and their eyes when they made contact with me could only be likened to the lion spotting the lamb. They salivated and breathed deeply while sharing knowing, sickly glances between themselves.

The small space was quickly full and I caught a flicker of concern flash between Van Ives and Vaughn. There were not enough seats so the newcomers stood, but that again was cause for unease. This felt calculated and that was never good.

"What is this? Who are these people?" Vaughn did a good job of holding the tone in his voice. He was still authoritative and calm, but my tingling senses were picking up on what his brain was doing and it didn't match up.

"These, Mr Vaughn, are my associates. The Venari has been operating for hundreds of years and this moment is significant to our history. We are the elders, the leaders of our organization and so, as you can imagine, there is much desire between them to see it come to pass." Seemed almost reasonable if that was how you could put it, but we all knew there was always more.

These were the crème de la crème of cult, the keepers of the secrets and descendants of the people who hung and killed those that went before me. The poster children of megalomania.

They leered and leaned, their body language a twist of lustful, greedy jeers.

"Very well. Let us finish this." Vaughn cleared his throat and cracked his intertwined fingers one by one with a simple stretch.

The two sides were eyeballing each other warily. I sat in the middle contemplating my expression. Was I looking worried enough, on edge? How does someone carry themselves when they have been sold off for use as a weapon of mass destruction? I kept my eyes down as much I could and allowed my body to slump in the seat. Defeated, that's how I looked.

"Shall we deal with the transfer?" Vaughn was very eager for a man who had no means to deliver on his promise. Van Ives had his hands gripped tight to the edge of the table and for the first time there was a trace of unease and it spiked my own. If I could sense it, so could they. They may have been asses but they were astute asses nonetheless.

I had been worried about the arrival of Sutcliffe's allies, but realistically whatever we chose to do next, it could only help if we had more of them to stop. These were the gatekeepers to a hate mission and to have them in one place was rare and unlikely to be repeated, well, hopefully after today a repeat would be impossible one way or another.

I could feel we were building to some sort of crescendo; there wasn't much ground left to cover and the moment was long established. It was kind of like careering downhill and seeing your only way across the void below was broken. You just had to hope you were moving fast enough to clear it and leave the rest to science, or fate, depending on your perspective.

Sutcliffe brought a steel briefcase from under the table and placed it gently on the cool, hard surface. He clicked open its latches, it was the only sound in the room, bar the relentlessness of my pulse which was thumping constantly in my ears. Inside the case was decked out in sleek, black technology.

"If you could just type in the account number from which you are transferring. We will receive an automated response which confirms the money has switched accounts and then you will be free to go."

Vaughn stared down at the buttons and all I could hear were tense, heavy breaths. It took me a moment to realize they were mine. He started typing. What the hell could he be typing? They didn't have hundreds of millions of Euros; that was for sure.

A high pitched beep sounded and Sutcliffe spun the case back round. His face was expressionless so I couldn't tell if the noise meant that it had worked or not. Still, how? How could it have possibly worked and what the hell was next? I don't know why between all of us, not one was able to get any clear handle on the end, how it happened. Maybe because it was so changeable, there were too many ways for it to play out; but one thing was for sure, it was freaking annoying to have all this power at my disposal but no way of simply watching it play out. Just a clue, that was all I wanted.

Within the time it took to blink Van Ives had dialed me in, engaged my brain with his and without even hearing the words I saw it, what they were doing. He was clueing me in. The money wasn't there, but between them there was enough power to alter the tech, to make it look, to all intents and purposes, like that the transfer had been successful. I liked their style. Made sense to finally be using all this to get some small pay back.

Sutcliffe eyed his cheerleading squad and the sea of suits stared back like Stepford Wives. He nodded and one of them, positioned slightly to the front, stepped forward. He was younger than the rest by probably ten or so years and slightly better built. He inched towards Vaughn and extended a hand. Van Ives stood up, wary and the hairs on my neck prickled like barbed wire on my skin. The air felt colder as tensions rose.

Vaughn stood to meet him and outstretched his own hand, then everything went into free-fall. As their hands met, the Venari stranger slid his other hand inside his jacket. It was like time had frozen and I was the only one who could see what was coming. His hand returned and in it a pistol. The steel glimmered under the artificial light. I wanted my voice to work fast enough, but it wouldn't. I was paralyzed when I most needed to act. I failed them. No sooner had he revealed it than he fired two shots in close succession. Vaughn, wide eyes let down his grip and clutched his stomach. A raised hand dripped with new, fresh crimson and he spluttered a breath as more surged through his parted lips. He slid lifelessly from his seat, his lungs bubbly and hissing with the blood.

I wasn't even screaming, I was just frozen. Van Ives. He was hit in the head and already down and dead, no lingering death at least. The realization didn't take long to come. The whole time they wanted the money and me. They never had any intention of letting me go to any bidder, they just wanted to see how much they could make from me and then take me away as their prisoner.

I fought my desire to be sick as I traced the intricate track of the dots Van Ives' blood had left on my hand; I started to lose myself to another sensation. One with which I was equally familiar but was similarly unwelcome. It had been days and I suppose it was no wonder that this absurd scenario would prompt it, but a vision was the last thing I wanted right now. The room darkened until I could see nothing but the tiniest pinhole of light as my body gave way to that sense of weightlessness that brought me to what I would see.

It was dark and hot. So, so hot. Wherever it was, it was cramped and uncomfortable. Then it hit like someone flicked a switch. This wasn't discomfort. There was searing pain working its way up from my feet. I couldn't move them, they were trapped. I was already waning, this was short and horrific and what was worse was it wasn't one of mine but I couldn't dive deep enough to get a sense for who it was. My mind was too busy and it reflected the fragility of the vision, I wasn't able to piece things together like normal. It was fragmented and uneven like a jigsaw with missing pieces. I tried to grasp on to the image, search for more but it was like holding on to the edge of a cliff with just your fingernails… painful, wearing and you knew it wouldn't last, that you would fall anyway but you had to try. And I did. I fell back into that room with the final part of the image etched in my mind. It was the outstretched hand of the body I had been witnessing and it wasn't so much the lifelessness but what it held. The fingers were wrapped around something which glistened as my mind whirled backwards towards my real life. It was like watching something as I lost gravity and drifted away, but it was not just something. Something wasn't the right word, this, this thing was everything and it painted a picture I couldn't even begin to entertain. The image of the tiny letter just dropping out of a clenched fist like a final note adrift on a sheet of music was too much.

I pleaded silently for it to be wrong, but I knew they never were. It was too much to hope that this could be some cruel error, that now I was losing my gifts, to call them that sounded sickening in these circumstances.

If that was his hand and that letter was my symbol falling from it then this was already over and that elusive time, the time at which I would bring about their own end, that was now. I didn't expect the feeling of intense grief to manifest itself in such a way. I endured the crushing of my lungs, the feeling of such intense compression that life itself should cease, but almost as soon as it came, it gave way to something else. Every nerve in my body was electrified with agony. It passed through my cells virulently and my fingers tingled.

The veritable floodgate of hidden emotion, the concealed rage and the power that surged through me, were unlocked as I thought of every word we had ever spoken, every moment of joy or confusion. The touch of his skin against mine, the taste of his lips. My mind spun through every sound we had heard together, the way my name sounded specifically when it left his lips and the smell at the base of his neck where it met his collarbone. If that was gone, if there was none of his blood pumping, if his heart was still and lifeless in his chest, then I was done and I had nothing left to lose. It was like I was on rails, there was no shifting course.

I looked to the room but it was like it wasn't me. I was burning, my every cell alive with a century's worth of vitriol, not just mine, but everyone who sacrificed and lost for them and their quest. Alice, her friends and those girls who started it all and burned for us. It was going to stop.

Everything swirled and it felt like I was in the eye of the storm; the room swaying and pulsating around me. Confused faces peered back at me and I watched with fascination as their expression changed to fear. A few of them knew something was coming before anything happened outside of my brain. I watched their eyes send the message back and their bodies jerk into action.

I pushed the air around the room, just by thought at first, but my hands started to conduct it like it was a personal symphony playing out my plans for them. Without even a glance, before the thought was even complete in my mind, the restraints I was bearing were glowing and shattered in a flash of blinding light. Shrapnel exploded like tiny razor sharp darts and the sound suggested there was some collateral damage. Papers I hadn't even acknowledged thrashed on the changing air like confetti and I remember that first day of school in Salem, before they defiled the life I knew and innocence I held. The memory only served to further agitate me and my body responded. I raised my hands above my head and the doors flew open and the glass wall in which they were set crackled as the glass splintered within its frame, depicting an angry, ever-increasing spider web. A chorus of panicked groans echoed through the rushing sounds and anther small herd, just two or three of the weaker ones battled over and around each other like rats to find their exit.

Sutcliffe wasn't moving. I didn't need to look at him, I could sense him to my left where he had been holding court moments before and now I was sure that he was looking on terrified of this, the monster he created with his own greed and that of a thousand others.

"You wanted to see what I could do." Tears were streaming down my face now but my speech wasn't broken or labored. The sound of my voice was different, like the vision had stripped me of everything I was clinging on to. I had become The One, The One they always talked about. I wasn't Scarlett at that moment, I was The One sent to end it all and this room was the setting for the events so long foretold. Terrifying power was building at my fingertips, my head burning with the weight of a thousand gifts I hadn't even exercised before.

Sutcliffe's eyes were wired now, wide open and a sliver of the light of his teeth showed through parted lips. They were engaged in a will to speak or scream but there was no sound coming out. I was about to show him.

Those who remained in the room were either fascinated or desperate to leave but this had certainly sorted out who was serious about their desire for power. The ones who still clung to morbid fascination even in the light of this gathering dark were the ones to be really frightened of. So committed to their own ends and domination of people or power or money that they weren't even afraid for their own safety; their humanity was gone and in its place remained a dark, dull hole where there should have been a soul.

The remaining Collective looked on, their eyes desperate and their desire for vengeance etched indelibly on their faces. They weren't just looking at me, they were looking to me for a solution. They were desperate with grief and anger. Their friends had been murdered in front of them in a quest to assist me. I owed them and I knew it.

My mind didn't need any more focus. I had a clearer

thought process now than I had ever had. Pain, that was a good motivator for me, we all knew that it was proving true. I felt the pull, the way my body drew power from them and it didn't matter that there were less than intended, I hardly needed it. I think I could have set off a nuclear winter the way I was feeling. To have love torn from your chest when it had become some inextricably linked with your being was incredibly motivating when the people that had caused, and were causing, all the horrors were standing right in front of you.

STORM

All eyes were firmly on me now and all other agendas were off. It was just me and them and they were keen to stay focused on me now, for different reasons.

I wanted to engage, to bring about the beginning of the end, but I was picking up on something not so close but still very relevant. I listened in on the more distant sounds in my brain. These sounds were residing in the twisting, gnarled paths on the outer edges of the maze of my thoughts but they were closing in to the epicenter; my present. Sirens. A hundred sirens. Then my brain whirled into action. They were here, coming here. Within twenty minutes there could be a hundred people from the emergency services and if I didn't derail them, chances were they would be coming down with us.

I pushed with all I had. My mind surged and I felt the echo of my power move beyond me, beyond the walls. I had never done the mind control thing with a view to going through more than one room but if it bought us just a little time it was worth it for me and them. Still locked within my head I waited until the shift happened. The sounds that threatened to approach dissipated, their planned presence derailed, for a while at least.

I barged my way through the room and with a flick of my hand discarded two or three of them that had been blocking the door and they swung dramatically back and into the wall with a thud. As I broke free from that confined room, my eyes searching, I was struck by the coolness of the air. The sound of my pacing feet against that same cold floor we had walked across, greater in numbers, just a short time before, echoed throughout the building.

My head felt as though it was on fire and I stretched and flexed my hands which were still eager to release the rising tide of emotion, but I had to find her, I had to reclaim something from this chaos.

I thought she must still be there, where the chair had been discarded when we abandoned that room. Obviously no one deemed her a threat anymore and as far as they were concerned she had served her purpose. I swung the door open with less than a glance and was stunned to see the room empty, but the wheelchair remained. I stood and considered what it meant but there were footsteps following my path into the main room as the ever inquisitive and endlessly desperate to remain in charge came behind me but I had wasted enough time.

"Sutcliffe. Is this what you wanted? A real show?" I paraded back through and found him behind his cronies, still remarkably stony faced in light of what happened. He stared blankly for a moment.

"Miss Roth, I think this is more than a little unnecessary."

"Unnecessary? There are dead men in there. You have been lying and manipulating for years and all that lies in your wake is death and pain. You typify everything that is wrong with this world and choosing to sell me, sell a person and then killing those who paid you money, another low blow and the final one."

"That sounds like a threat." His voice didn't waver. I didn't allow mine to either.

"Maybe it is. I know this may be hard for you to comprehend but you don't know everything. Sometimes I have questioned it too, but finally, finally..." I couldn't even finish, didn't want to. My arms rose with the pressure that built in my head and a low, slow rumble reverberated through the floor. He looked to his feet, now unstable on the quaking ground and looked back to me, eyes wide. You could almost hear him processing, seeing the penny dropping. This was me and he wasn't ready for it.

"I see you've found your confidence, Miss Roth. Well, I am glad, it was always the idea that we would see what you could really do. Please... continue." The trepidation in his voice declared to all that he was bluffing, but it was always surprising how well he held things together.

Some of the others were not looking so confident. There were more than a few concerned glances and hushed exchanges behind Sutcliffe. They wanted to run so badly, but pride was a weakness for them and I enjoyed watching them squirm. I knew it was wrong, to take pleasure in anyone's discomfort, even if it was them, but I couldn't help it.

The ground groaned and creaked beneath our feet and I smiled back at him, the kind of smile he had always reserved for me; one filled with the promise of taking control.

"My pleasure." The images ingrained into my mind, his outstretched hand and the light of a flame reflecting on the silver S of my bracelet was enough to really get things going. My brain wouldn't stop imagining the rest of the vision, the parts I didn't see. What if I pulled him out? What if I was going to have to hold him as the life drained from him? The idea of watching his chest become still as the soul seeped from him to leave only the beautiful façade of him. I was suffocated by the agony. It clung to my lungs and wrapped itself around them like black, creeping vines, slithering and twisting until there was nothing but a mass of knots and tangles which could never be undone.

I brushed the air with my right hand and a crack splintered across the polished stone floor and forked angrily toward where they stood just a few feet away. The sea of feet danced and hopped away but I simply watched the lines being drawn and pushed them closer. When the web had been woven, a vibration so low and deep surged through the ground and the cracks widened until huge chunks of the floor fell into the open, cavernous foundations below. Within seconds I was standing on the only untouched piece of ground for twenty feet. They retreated into the direction of a corridor of rooms much like the one where Van Ives and Vaughn lay dead and I forced them further still as the opening ground chased them back.

A small, less confident faction backed off to the right into the waiting doorway of another room and I slammed the door, separating them and their now audible screams of panic from this space. Terrified fists thumped and punched at the wood on the other side.

My head was swimming with the possibilities, anger, my own fear and, strongest of all, grief. I remembered what I had taken from my time in Amsterdam and I set another two down, turning off their brains like computers in hibernation. Watching bodies fall, lifeless to the floor was terrifying and electrifyingly exciting all at once. I knew they were fine, but he didn't. To all intents and purposes, they were expired and I had been the one to do it.

With numbers dwindling, Sutcliffe was tense. It was subtle, little things that gave him away. The small, circular motion between his index finger and thumb, the tiny movement of tensing jaw muscles behind his whiskery stubble. If there was safety in numbers, he was more unsettled than ever. These were his highest ranking and they were falling or bailing on him.

I had considered stepping down. Using his fear as my cue to warn him and leave, but that wasn't what history taught us, it wasn't what Alice had told me. To end this, it had to really be over, but until that moment he had still been left with some chance. Until he spoke again.

"Very good. I'm impressed. Such a shame Mr Mayer isn't here to see this. He was always one of the best. The most'committed'." He meant Mayer Senior and even the mention of him still sent chills down my spine.

"Well, I am so sorry for your loss. But he was a spiteful, evil man and you and all the rest of them deserve everything that is coming. It's true… at one point I thought all of this..." I gestured to the beginning of the destruction around us, "was unnecessary. I believed there had to be a way, a peaceful resolution. That perhaps if we showed you that we, The Collective were good, could do good, it might be different. But the more I watch you, the more I see, the worse it gets. It never even started out as fear, it was eradication of the different, the unusual and a desperate need to maintain a hierarchy and conformity. There was never hope for us."

"We don't seek conformity, Miss Roth, we simply seek to eradicate that which has no place in the natural order. If this was how we were supposed to be, it would be your side that were the majority, but alas, you remain a small, extinguishable force."

"Extinguishable? Do you think so little of human life? Do you care for nothing?"

He laughed, slowly. It built into a deep, throaty, maniacal laugh which echoed through the corridor. "I care for a great deal; namely the restoration of our race into one free of abominations like you and your friend Alice."

"Why? Because you feel threatened by the capabilities or because you hate to be the one without the power?"

"Without the power? Your very being here is by my design." He stepped around a huge opening in the floor and casually kicked in a piece of rubble from his wake. "We have systematically wiped out the most powerful of your kind for years. Keeping the order and never once drawing unnecessary attention to our organization. I would say that suggests we have more than our fair share of power, wouldn't you?"

"But what have you actually achieved? I see death, sure, but here we are, you and I, and if your interest in me stems from the very lore you have followed to find me, then you know this only ends one way. I'm The One." It felt strangely empowering to say it out loud and it was the first time I had truly believed it. I was crying again, aching for Jake and wanting to make this right. I wished over and over to be able to change the course, change what was happening but I was on a ride and I couldn't get off it now.

"Yes... I would agree perhaps we underestimated you, but you're still here and so am I, so no one should be hanging up the flags just yet, Miss Roth." He clicked his fingers and one of the few remaining stepped forward. Those trapped were still causing a commotion in the room beyond and the noise grated me. I clicked my own fingers and silence befell us all. Sutcliffe tipped his head in a strange kind of way, like he was almost congratulating me. A silent touché.

The wide-eyed stranger stepped cautiously forward and handed Sutcliffe a phone. He in turn, passed it to me.

"What do you want me to do with this? Is there someone you want to call before we finish this?" I surprised myself, less by what I had said and more because I meant it.

"On the contrary. I thought you may have someone you wanted to call. Jake Mayer, perhaps?" He smirked as he clocked the reactions on my face. A response to the knife in my gut as I thought of his hand desperately reaching outwards, bloody and clutching my name.

"Don't you dare speak his name." I took a step towards him, navigating over the unstable ground.

"Oh, so sour all of a sudden. We were having such a nice chat. No final words for your Prince Charming?" He skirted around the gaping hole between us and looked at his watch. "I am surprised. You know, I almost feel a little guilty. Tearing young love apart this way. Pulling you from the arms of him after all you've been through. If there was a way to simply wipe out the unnaturalness of what you can do, I may have been tempted."

"You would never have offered that as an option. The power trip would have been that bit less if you just let me walk, surely?" A lump threatened in my throat. If only it had been an option; I would have snapped their hand off. Why couldn't it be that way? Why wasn't one of my powers the ability to change time? I should have been grateful for what I did have, the power to change history; I knew that was the greater gift but my selfishness led me to care only for him. Either way the catalyst existed, whether or not that was the right one was kind of irrelevant, it just needed to do the job.

"I guess we will never know now, will we, Miss Roth? Instead, what have you achieved? You have squandered every opportunity we have ever provided for cooperation."

I couldn't contain my horrified laughter. "Opportunity? You have never posed any opportunity for me, bar what method of torture I would choose to die by." He tutted as he shook his head and his nonchalant attitude was the final straw. I thrust my attention at the floor alongside him. The hairline cracks widened and a further section of floor fell away. He stumbled as his foot teetered on the brink of the chasm.

A guttural scream, the months and years of pent up anger and confusion I had felt since they found me. What they put me through in that hell hole of an asylum and everything since. Torture. Pain. Anxiety. Fear and the worst of all, loss. They had to pay for mine and for everyone else's. Alice was missing, presumed dead. Jake, I could only guess was here somewhere ready to be consumed by the carnage. Stubborn ass. Why hadn't he stayed where I had told him?

As ever, thinking of Jake made me feel funny, but this time, for the first time it wasn't the good kind. I clung to the chasm of desperation that was gaping within me and I was going to use it. I was going to rain hell down on this man and his merry monsters once and for all. Now.

I didn't say another word. I didn't even want to. I poured every single fiber of my being, every strand of DNA into what I was about to do.

The rumble returned with a kind of ferocity I hadn't even dared to dream and I still had an arsenal. I was almost scared of myself. My skin started to burn red hot and it radiated from every pore to the point where my, usually pale, skin had an almost ethereal glow. The heat was driven to my outstretched hands, and directly to my fingertips. The heat was so intense it almost made me cry out in pain, but I channeled it and lined up my hands with the view I had of Sutcliffe. I imagined them around his neck as he stared back at me and if I half closed my eyes it looked within my line of sight like my burning fingers were grasping either side of his neck. Every desire I had ever had for vengeance spewed from my mind and the sensation was so real I could feel the gritty, splintered texture of his skin pebble dashed with course stubble. I let the feeling sink in and imagine what it would be like to press my fingers into that skin like he had to mine on several occasions. I imagined my fingernails digging in, breaking his skin and releasing the pressure I had been harboring for so long. I was frightened; it felt good.

Sutcliffe stared back at me amid the building's groans as its foundations were tested by the field of force that was slowly building around me. The spinning sensation was back and with it a host of other goodies for my audience; many of whom were finally starting to look like they were regretting their quest to hunt me down. Good, was all I could think.

His face still twisted in his sick satisfaction he wouldn't back down. I pushed harder mentally and something changed. The more realistically I could feel his skin beneath my fingertips, the wider his eyes got. The smirk slowly slid away until his eyes were gaping and he started to clutch his throat for the breath I had stolen. Twisting harder I watched as my mime of inflicting pain on him played out with perfect accuracy.

As he groped for breath he forced another smirk but the sincerity was lost, he was scared. "Wonderful to see you working your... magic. Witch." He hissed the words through strained breath, his own hands still grabbing at the imaginary force around his neck. He released his grip and with a brief, lightning quick motion, beckoned one of the onlookers forward, but his minions were not as gutsy as he and they were reluctant. "Now."

The sharp shooter from earlier appeared from behind a quaking, crumbling stone pillar as chunks of thick plaster and ceiling tiles started to litter the area like huge, threatening confetti. He pulled the gun with impressive speed and took a shot. I felt the slowing of time as I watched the bullet leave the gun and without flinching I twisted the air around it as it flew and altered its path to curve away from its intended target. I flashed him the kind of smile Sutcliffe reserved for me and with little more than a look I tossed the gun from his hand and we watched in unison as it skidded through the debris and coursed down the broken floor into a waiting trench. The gunslinger looked at Sutcliffe and shook his head, he was out. He turned to run but I couldn't let the man who shot those innocent people just walk away, or scuttle, that was a better word.

I hopped over the crack beyond my feet which was growing with every passing second and glanced upwards as another hunk of ceiling fell with a crash to the floor sending up more dust into the turbulence that was my making. It paved the way for me to reach him and the crunch of my feet on the rubble was a satisfying sound to carry me forward. He continued to back away but stumbled over a crack and landed with an ungraceful thud.

"Need to be a little more careful there." I stopped a couple of feet short of him and reveled in his squirming. He tried to make it back to his feet but I made sure he couldn't stand. His wide, terrified eyes pleaded but his voice was too proud. He threw a protective arm up over his face and I could see he was already broken, no further threat. He was in too deep and he knew it. I turned to step away and focus on Sutcliffe, who by this point had repositioned himself defensively against a wall which hadn't yet shown signs of strain.

"Weak. Witch bitch." Whispered a voice behind me. My friend obviously felt his ego was wounded by his previous cowardice. Weak? No. I blinked the next step into action before my nerves had even snapped together.

The TVs in the room beyond flickered to life and crackled and popped before disappearing into a plume of gray smoke and sparks. As eyes turned to see what had happened, the deep rumble beneath the floor turned to a louder, roar and things started to collapse around us. In the distance sparks turned to the glow and crackle of flames.

"What did you call her?" The voice was changed and

my brain had to slow down from its erratic state of chaos to process it. My eyes darted from the fallen shooter to Sutcliffe and back to the remnants of the crowd. I couldn't hone in. I spun at speed seeking the owner, desperate to place it. Then she was just there.

The hunched, frail person I had last seen in the chair was upright, albeit just. She winced through the pain of standing straight and set her jaw as her hands matched mine. She raised them up and the force that emanated was like nothing I'd ever known and that was taking into account the events of the last few hours. Next to me, Alice was the most powerful of all of us, that's why she was the unfortunate one tasked with being their witchcraft sniffer dog for God knows how long.

Years of unspoken gratitude I didn't even know I had needed flowed from me and the air between us fizzed and spat with sparks and raw, terrifying energy. The temperature around us went from searing hot to ice cold so much so that I could see my breath. Dazzling, bright crystals of ice started to creep like fog up the walls and the ceiling, decorating the dull, fear drenched space with a rare kind of beauty that, if it had been anywhere else, would have taken my visible breath away.

When the walls were draped in a sheet of sweeping, icy glow I made my way to Alice and reached for her hand. She stepped over the cracks; the distant rumbling representing the storm building within me was still there.

As my fingers made contact with her hand I grasped it tighter than I have ever held anything before. The contact was matched with a thunderclap so loud The Collective members looked afraid and they were right to be so. Small chunks of plaster were replaced with huge, hulking blocks, the building started to melt around us, slices of wall sliding off into clouds of rubble and dust that made the air thick and heavy.

They started to run, to disperse the way animals flock before a natural disaster, which was kind of appropriate. Sutcliffe wouldn't give in to his pride though, ever. I motioned for Vaughn's friends to run, there wasn't going to be any more innocent blood spilled for me.

Alice wasn't done though, quite rightly she had her own agenda after her years spent in their servitude. She looked to the shooter, his eyes too scared to meet hers and she twisted a hand in the air towards him. His body writhed in pain, she was tapping into my powers, we were sharing the energy and she was executing her will through my power. He turned and contorted, his spine arched unnaturally until he was nearly bent double. His screams almost matched the sounds of the collapse and chaos surrounding us. When he was literally about to break I pulled her arm to her side.

"He isn't worth it. You're better than him." A silent, single tear rolled down her face and she released her invisible grip. He fell silent but his face was still twisted with agony.

DESTRUCTION

As the remaining crowd scattered I felt Alice's brain click into action. With all I could do coursing through her veins, she brought a section of ceiling down on the path of the Venari deserters with less than a look. She trapped them with us in the space. We didn't discuss it, we didn't need to. We were both willing to do whatever it took; neither of us felt like anything selfish was enough to justify letting them walk. We would stay, together, until we knew it was over.

Sutcliffe was the lynchpin; he was going down with this ship no matter what.

With a silent agreement, we both closed our eyes. I felt

the air pick up pace as it turned and twisted around us. From one second to the next it spun into a furious hurricane so fierce I struggled to keep my feet on the ground. We anchored each other and watched as Sutcliffe was tossed and dropped like a weakened branch. He landed in a tangled heap and we stepped towards him, pausing for a falling block. The room was barely standing. So much had fallen from the floor above that we could see two, maybe three, stories up. A pin-hole shard of light appeared in the wall to my right as an external wall started to give. The sound was unbelievable. The steel fame of the building curving and bowing was like a freight train on the move only louder and warmer. All the energy coming off it was being absorbed by us. Alice and me, we were drawing all the power from everything into our clasped hands and pushing it right back at him. It was hot now, the former icy cobwebs dripped into the dust below.

The hiss of exposed wires grew louder as sparks danced into flames that licked the ceiling from the exposed cavities between floors. The heat was searing but we were invincible, it was as if we were radiating something to keep it at bay. The others were starting to splutter and writhe with discomfort as the temperature rose and the flames crept ever higher. They peeled off their expensive suits which were worthless now and they turned to each other in desperation.

We stood above Sutcliffe, a heap of long limbs slumped

against a now unstable wall. He looked up at us, defiantly; he still had enough arrogance to let a little tooth show between his lips. Alice still clung to me, she wasn't strong enough to stand alone but I sensed she was taking as much from our union as I was. She was bolstered by it enough to stand with me.

"So, now what? You're united and you intend to exact some bloody revenge on me, is that it?" He forced an irritating laugh, but it came from his throat, not his gut. It was pretense.

"We never wanted blood. We never wanted any of this." I wanted it all to disappear.

"Yet here we are and we know we can't, or should I say won't, all be leaving here in one piece. I have invested my life to bringing these atrocities to a rightful conclusion and despite this rather, elegant spectacle of yours... I am not going to walk away. So, what was that about blood shed?" He wanted to push me; he was challenging me to kill him knowing that I could never live with blood on my hands, no matter how toxic. He wiped a smear of blood from his lips with a casual motion and examined the resulting stain on the back of his kind.

"I don't need to kill you. It just isn't my job to save you." Alice was already pulling on my hand, she was getting weaker. We stepped away, our backs turned.

"Oh, come on." The grit grated and ground beneath his feet as he tried to stand. I bit my lip, frightened to take the next step, so I just let myself breathe. "I really didn't think it would be this easy. I hoped the little girl lost would die with your hope and some of the real fight would come out, not just the show and tell skit." Without looking I felt the air move before I heard the sound of the safety on the gun. I didn't need the millisecond it took to click.

She was around before my brain had even processed it and with a movement so slight she cast the gun from his hand with the piercing crack of the bone in his forearm. His wail echoed through the smoke and heat and the others cowered, their faces now black with the soot. Sprinklers poured water over us all, streaking the black dirt down us, mapping our time in that strange place on our clothes and on our faces.

"She might not want your blood on her hands, but I am ready to accept whatever the next life brings me. It can't be anything worse than I have endured in this." A tiny flex of her right index finger and some of the wall he was leaning on tumbled across him, trapping his legs. "Burn." Her voice was angry and pointed in a way I had never heard before. He was wailing like a wounded animal, his agony etched on his face. But the empathy, or guilt I might normally have felt simply melted away when I saw the relief on her face. She felt free, we were free.

We started to navigate a path back through to the main entrance where, hours before, my bidders had walked. As we moved away we shared a glance, another, unspoken agreement and she gave me the encouragement I needed.

We heard the result as the ceiling gave way in the space we had left them. I drowned out the sounds and the feelings and just focused on making it to the air outside. A huge blast shoved us forward and we careered across the floor, coursing through rubble as a fireball surged through the rooms we had been occupying. Fragments of plaster and floor tile were jaggedly hanging from one of my forearms and blood dripped from me. Alice was grazed and stunned but nothing we couldn't handle. The flames pushed their way towards us at speed and like I had done only once before, I used all I had to stop it in its tracks. My outstretched hand halted its path and instead of gorging on the oxygen in the foyer where we lay, it moved sideways in either direction. Alice smiled at me, like a proud grandmother might look upon a granddaughter who had excelled in her craft.

The air outside was cool and clean. My lungs grabbed every breath as I pulled Alice along with me, her legs were too tired now to bear even her frail weight, and laid her down on the concourse outside the building. She threw her arms around me and she sobbed.

"It wasn't a waste. You showed them. You brought the end of them."

"Only with your help." I cried on her, huge body-wracking sobs and all of my pent-up emotion spewed out like a geyser.

"Maybe that was it all along. Maybe that was my place too." She gasped. Her chest tight with smoke inhalation as her already fragile state, further compromised by today's events, started to struggle.

My body dared to almost relax when a feeling of utter horror washed over me. How could I have forgotten? How could I have not thought? I lay Alice down and gave her my top layer on which to rest her head. She was already losing consciousness but I had to go. I stood up and ran as fast my legs would carry me. There was pain rising from my ankles to my thigh bones from injuries I hadn't even acknowledged, but I pushed through it because I had left them there and they needed me.

I stopped in the foyer, more of the building was compromised now and through the state my emotions were in, I could feel the impact that my just being there was having. There was so much raw energy in me that it was finding a way out with every step. Each of my footprints was like taking one of the foundations away. Things were crumbling, swaying and every time my shoes hit the floor they were echoed by a ripple effect of tiny cracks. I was a walking bomb, I needed to calm down. I swung a left, to avoid having to see Sutcliffe or any of the rest of them, if they were even visible anymore, under the haze of smoke and flames.

I shielded my face from the heat as I stumbled through debris-littered corridors. The mess cleared and the pace of my beating heart dissipated somewhat as I created distance between me and the epicenter where The Venari were trapped. All the rooms I searched were empty. I looped back on myself but the pressure was building. I knew sections of this part of the building were too weak to last. I wasn't going to bring down a structure this size, but there was enough damage here for me to not want to stay.

I was breathless now and breathing through sobs. Where were they? My mind was clouded, I couldn't clear it enough to work logically. This was the problem, not being a political or evil mastermind I couldn't work through all this systematically when people I love were at risk, my focus fell to them.

As if he was waiting until I needed him I felt the push, the arrival of Elias' voice in my head.

Thank God. Elias, where are you? Mom?

Scarlett, we just got outside. The room we were in started to fill with smoke through the air vents, so I broke up and out. I couldn't reach you but I could tell some serious crap was going down. Get out of here.

Ok. I'm coming.

I desperately retraced my steps and the pain that seared into me as I made my way outside was as intense as anything I had ever known. How my feet went one in front of another I had no idea. I was weighed down with fragility. Was Jake here, now, awaiting a fate I had created for him? Should I stay and look or resign myself to the fact I had never been able to derail one vision before and focus on who I had saved, how could he be saved? I didn't intend to scream, but it didn't wait for permission, it broke forth from my heaving lungs and I slumped against a wall, allowing it to possess me entirely. I had never screamed so loud, or so real, in my life. There was always that stigma attached to real fear or pain; we are all so busy being polite and considerate that we rarely allow ourselves to let go but to walk out of this building, which may already have consumed him, taken him from me, was beyond every definition of impossible I could every envisage.

Scarlett. Leave. Now.

Elias wasn't messing around. He might have known something I didn't, it was like I was functioning at one hundred percent. I wiped my face and scraped my hollow body from the floor before stumbling out towards where I left Alice. The pain in my legs suddenly felt a lot more real and the last few steps felt like the onset of death when coupled with the ache in my chest.

Through eyes drowning in tears I could only see the shapes of them. They were on the grass with water beyond. This place should have been beautiful, this incredible feat of modern engineering, bordered by water... it was a modern day castle occupied by dragons.

My mom was black with soot from the fire, but there were no other discernible injuries that I could see. She was hysterical upon seeing me and practically dragged me down to the ground with her. I broke again even though I didn't think there were any pieces of me left that hadn't been shattered or tainted with sadness. We just lay for a while a tangle of gratitude, love, grief, relief and so many more that were indiscernible in the chaos. The building still groaned beyond us and we were stunned to attention by the shattering of glass in the foyer as the heat put them through.

With some of my focus back, I passed my eyes over my mom again to check for blood, but still none, well, nothing more than a few scratches and bruises. Alice was on her back, her arm draped over her face. My heart stopped for a moment when I couldn't discern any notable rise and fall in her chest, but it was there, just. My mom moved to her and took her hand and I watched as she passed her thumb over Alice's wrist. It was such a small gesture, one so many people would have done, but it was just my mom and I tried to remember how lucky that had made me and still made me. She was something I had to keep my focus for, even if right now it didn't feel that she was enough and the shame of that was just another nail in my heavy chest.

The realization that something was missing was slow at first, then as subtle as a sledgehammer. Elias. Where was he?

There was no connection. The line was well and truly dead.

"Mom... where is Elias? Wasn't he with you?" Her face

fell, like the joy of our being reunited had clouded her mind too and she wasn't thinking clearly, albeit for different reasons.

"Ah… he, he… stayed inside, said he wanted to find you and then he sent me here." Her voice started to quiver as she saw the words seep into my consciousness. "Scarlett… don't. Please."

But I had already pushed myself to my feet and started another loop back towards the building. I was half way across the concourse when I saw some more of the foyer's ceiling collapse and it set off a chain reaction of pounding, thunderous sounds as more and more of it fell out of view but I felt it through the ground. Getting back in there was more dangerous but it was like I had no regard anymore. I had to save anyone who could be saved.

I pushed and pushed to force the line open but it was white noise. I stepped through sharp splinters of glass and angry almost sculpture-like piles of rubble with protruding steel to find some more rooms to search. The white noise continued but its strength ebbed and flowed and it took me some time to recognize that it was like a beacon. Even with the line down I could hone in on the energy, the closer I got, the louder the sound became.

Three, four rooms and nothing, then suddenly the frequency was right. I was just one set of partition walls away from the eye of the storm and I could hear the faint coughs and cries of The Venari on the other side. I had to not care, I had to focus.

"Scarlett... it still isn't over." Sutcliffe growled the words and I could hear them over all of the madness. He was still getting to me, even now, but his voice was all the energy he had, I could feel it lacked the substance he usually gave but in the state I was in the sound of his voice was an unwelcome mix and the precursor to an unwelcome reaction. I didn't reply but the things I wanted to say, the things I thought about doing to him, were represented by a torrent of tumbling walls, panels of political boardrooms falling one by one like some disastrous domino run. When the destruction took out the wall in the room next to me the signal was boosted and the white noise became almost deafening. I was close. I trod lightly over the threshold into the next room and found myself almost down to my hands and knees to traverse the broken desks damaged by the collapsed ceiling. It wasn't here though, he wasn't here.

The scene was like something from a superhero movie, where the bad guy's juggernaut of a henchman had smashed the place to smithereens, only I was technically the henchman in this scenario. It was hard to reconcile that this was me but a glimpse into my own thoughts and the feelings I had experienced when I heard his voice was enough to bring it all home; this destruction, it was all me.

The dust, broken glass, metal and leather from plush office furniture littered the floor, once trodden by supposedly great men and women committed to the advancement of the modern world and now I was here because they had attempted to lead it in a direction that screwed it all up instead.

Déjà vu. My vision rippled with recognition until my sight was focused on a pile of broken ceiling tiles balancing precariously on top of a dilapidated supporting wall, now just a heap of heavy, hulking lumps of concrete and plaster.

The sound was painful now and I ran a finger along the bottom of my ear to catch the droplet of blood that was about to trail down and trace my jawline as my eyes met the thing I thought I knew.

This was what I had seen but all at once the sound I was hearing was too much to bear. The slightest turn of my head revealed the glimmer I recognized; the glinting light from a partially wrecked fluorescent lamp which hung twisted and bent but still connected to its source of power was catching it as I knew it would, as I had seen it before this time was to come.

I had thought about this endlessly, painfully, experienced the feeling that my very soul was pouring from invisible wounds as a result, but nothing was even close to preparation for the reality. The swell of agony in my chest felt like it might just burst open and leave me part of the vast wreckage; another piece of collateral damage.

My feet defied every other sensation I was experiencing and pointed me towards the light. I knelt close to it and swept away a rogue tile which blocked the part I knew I could never be ready to see. With a limp, dusty hand exposed I broke completely to the point my breath was all but gone… choked from my chest by horror and a desire to be anywhere but in that room.

My hand was shaking like all that flowed through my veins was pure adrenalin but I checked for the pulse I knew I wouldn't find and before my hand could leave the cold skin I was caught up in a frantic rescue mission. There was no mad scramble and dragging the weight of the chaos away piece by piece; instead I put the pain to better use and a few pointed sweeps of my palms sent the debris shooting away from us in every direction until the very last piece which obscured his face. That was the part that halted me. Dead.

I tugged the last piece of rubbish away as slowly as I could but my current state was pushing the already failing building to its limit and I was next if I didn't move soon. His face.

Ashen, cold and devoid of everything I had ever seen in it. How the hell had this happened? The bracelet? This room? The chain of events, the vision, it was all a blur. I cried for him, more tears than before and allowed the pain in my lungs and throat to pass beyond the ache into the rare kind of pain that people are not supposed to face at this stage in their life. Seeing someone's final place, the end of a human, was something I didn't ever think I would see so close. I dragged my arm across my face to clear the dust and tears away; I could feel it heavy and claggy on my skin. I felt aged through experience and my body through exhaustion but I buried it, like I had so many other things and I needed to get him out, he couldn't lie with them; this was not his resting place. He deserved so much better.

Dead weight was one of those phrases people throw around, with, in most cases, a pleasing lack of experience to understand what it actually means. Pulling him out of there amidst the heat, the cries and the threat of continued collapse only worsened by my reaction to his body was one of the hardest things I had ever done. Feeling skin I had experienced warm now rest on mine but with the cool residue of death was soul destroying. At least most of my soul was gone already creating a shorter distance to fall.

His body kept snagging on the jagged debris and in the end it was my powers that helped me break him free of that place. I pushed and moved him with my mind but I couldn't touch him anymore, the emptiness of a body without breath, and devoid of all sense of the things that made us connect, made the weight of him too much. The struggle was beyond the physical, all of me was floundering now.

When I got outside every inch of the wall within me broke down and the parts of me I was holding on to crumbled and gave way. Everything I had seen, everything I had done and heard, was dissolving me from the within. So I let go. I was out, they were in. I had carried this body into the cool air as the sun was setting on the water behind where I had left Mom and Alice. Someone was with them but the sun's light obscured the view.

I made it no more than half way to them before the third shadow started running towards me. I had lost it, so I thought, because I felt too weak to believe that anything good might happen.

I closed my eyes as the gap between us closed. Already on my knees with the relief, the guilt that relief brought me while Elias lay dead at my feet. Then his arms enveloped me and I fell into every waiting emotion. I wasn't even crying anymore, I was gasping for breath like the sight of him had brought me back from the brink of drowning; which I guess it had.

"Don't cry, Scarlett, Shh. It's ok. It's ok now, I'm here." His arms enveloped me and I felt the warmth I had worried for so long I would never feel again. I collapsed onto him as he knelt beside me and brushed the dust knotted hair from my face. "Blood. Is this...? Are you bleeding?" His eyes searched me frantically for damage. All I could think was that there was so much damage and most of it was concealed.

"No. No. it's not mine. It's..." my voice trailed off and my eyes took the weight of the rest of the sentence. I cast my eyes to Elias lying lifeless on the ground with his stupid floppy black hair covering his face. There was blood seeping from a wound on his forehead that snaked down past his nose and pooled on his lips.

"Oh Christ... is he?" Jake stumbled backwards "No... NO!" He surged forward and started crude, angry CPR on his chest. His hands balled into fists he pounded against Elias's chest again and again. I had never heard that sound before but I knew it would never leave me.

"Come on. No. No." Jake was losing his breath, he was pushing so hard but you could see there was no comeback. Elias was gone. The stupid jackass had lied. He had managed to pull the wool over my eyes and in a flash I heard his last words all over again. Get out of here. Not get out of there, he knew he was trapped and he was trying to send me out to safety. How had I missed that?

"Jake. Jake stop. He's gone." Jake rocked back onto his knees and let his head fall into his hands. He had hated Elias at times but somewhere in there, they liked each other, respected each other and shared a love for me. That would always win, they would put aside any difference in the world to keep me safe and I loved them both for it in different ways. Elias was the most unlikely best friend I could have ever asked for. He was stubborn, overly aggressive, rude and intrusive at times but when he cared he did it fiercely and without expectation. He was a good person, a great one and he shouldn't have died in that place.

"Why did you come? I thought it was you." My lungs lurched as though they were threatening to leave my throat and grab at the air themselves.

"Thought what was me?" He pulled me to him and embraced me in such a way that spoke a thousand words. I had always, through all of this minimized his feelings, made out like this was the hardest for me as I was the one going into the fray, but I was selfish and naïve to ignore his love for me that way. Whether it was a defense mechanism or not, a hint that I still didn't feel like I was worthy of the same kind of feelings back from him, I didn't know, but everything he had felt since we had been apart was clear in the way he held me in that moment.

The building was still alive with sound. It was glass and heat crackling and minor collapses every few seconds and we both flinched as another thud echoed from the smoking structure. The flames that raged deep in the bowels of the building had started to lick at the open wounds in the exterior.

"Why did he have this? How?" I held out the bracelet to him. Jake eyed it and a faint smile washed over his face, which was otherwise gray with the proximity of death. He reached out and took it from me. He bit his lip as he wrestled with the tiny clasp and put it around my wrist; making it the one beautiful thing about me with my blood stained, dirty skin and ripped clothes.

"I came before. I broke in when you were in the main room. I found your mom and Elias. He flipped out, went crazy at me for not listening. Kept saying how mad you would be, how hurt if anything happened to me and that I was a jerk for disrespecting your wishes."

"Yeah. That sounds like him. And he was right. You were a jerk for ignoring me." I pulled him to me and let his lips part mine. "But, I am so glad you're here."

"So I said I would leave. Wait somewhere else if he promised to give you this. I told him I trusted him and that I wanted him to bring you back to me. And he did."

I said I couldn't bear the thought of him being cold, so Jake lay his hoodie gently over Elias. Oh God, Ava. I would need to get word to her. How do you tell someone their big brother is dead? What will she think of me for bringing him into this?

I cried quietly for a while, my tears created a dark patch on Jake's gray shirt and he just held me, the way only he knew how. Close enough I felt safe but still with room to breathe. The perfect way.

"Mom. I need to go to Mom." Jake nodded and motioned for me to press on without him. In my periphery I saw the softness with which he scooped up Elias in his arms, the ease with which he raised him. I was proud of them both.

Mom was crying when we got there. "Elias? Is he?"

I just nodded, every word threatened to tip me over another, as yet unforeseen, precipice of reaction to it and the truth was I wasn't sure how I could keep falling over those edges and just keep breathing.

She looked solemnly to the side, her eyes heavy with

tears and faced the ground. Alice's arm had fallen limply from where it had been draped over her face and she was still again, like before only less hunched. I knew without checking because all of a sudden I felt like death and I were old buddies, like I could see his work everywhere and certainly feel it. More sadness befell me but it was different with Alice and I knew it would be selfish to want things another way. She held on for so long and it was time. She was ready. I knew that even without the chance to say a proper goodbye and I couldn't ignore the blissful peace in her expression. It brought a little peace to me, too, knowing that I had finally met her, embraced her and been there in her final moments to prove to her that everything she sacrificed for me was not in vain.

I draped my shirt over her even though the evening air was too cool to be in just a T. I wanted to cover her, let her rest now. Jake slid between me and Mom and put his arms around us both and without hesitation we leaned in to him for warmth, comfort and all three of us cried silent tears of relief.

A huge crash echoed around us and a burst of flame flew from the ailing building. A huge section of the edifice collapsed inwards and a thirty foot plume of dust and smoke filled the air.

"We need to leave, get out of here." Jake looked to me. I nodded.

"We need to get some word out on this, a message to the

rest of them and something to, well, make this look a little more normal to the rest of the blissfully ignorant." He pulled out his phone and stared at me before tapping something into the key pad.

"Jean, it's me. Yeah, yeah, Scarlett is fine. I can't go into everything now but we need to start leaving a trail… something that makes this whole thing look like an accident happened, maybe an electrical fault that started a fire. You're up, buddy? Yep, ok. I'll explain everything else later. We will speak soon." He pulled out the sim card from the cell and snapped the tiny rectangle in two before stamping on the handset and tossing it into the waiting water, the habit of trying to cover our tracks would take time to lose, if ever.

"Done. Now, let's get you two safe."

"What about them?" My mom made a great point.

"We lay them together, so they aren't alone. Of all the people in the world that would want us to get the hell out of here, it is these two." I knelt down at Elias's side and brushed that stupid hair from his face for the last time. "Goodbye, Elias. You crazy, angry, too busy pretending he doesn't care about anything ass. I'll carry your sense of fight and your passion with me always. I love you."

Jake saw the silent tears. He felt my pain and for the first time I think he really got it. He knew Elias wasn't a threat, just an incredible friend and someone unlucky enough in the end to know me and understand me. He had deserved better than I gave him. The profound sense of failure I felt as I stood staring as his lifeless body sent me into some kind of shock. My limbs quivered and I stabilized myself momentarily.

We knew we needed to haul ourselves as far away as possible but in a moment which touched me immeasurably, Jake paused our escape. He knelt back down alongside Elias and gently placed his hand in his own. "I don't have the words. I never will. Thank you for doing what I couldn't, for being what I wasn't and for keeping your promise. I'm sorry for being an ass to you." We didn't need to add anything else. It was his own goodbye and he needed it.

We stood in unison, my mom limping and pressing her weight onto Jake and me slightly behind. I turned as another series of windows blew and thought of what we were leaving behind in there.

Death. More loss. Blood being shed was never my intention, in fact, I felt sick even at the thought, but I did the only things I could. I made the choices I believed were right and once I moved away from feelings of guilt there was some strange poetic justice in the events which I saw unfold. We went full circle in that place. Burned at the stake, crushed with stone. They wrote the story and foretold their own demise without ever realizing.

The End.

CPSIA information can be obtained at www.ICGtesting.com
Printed in the USA
LVOW11s1432120615

442281LV00001B/41/P